I0460932

CAUGHT IN THE MOMENT

Freefall, Book 1

Brandy Walker

Caught in the Moment, Freefall, Book One

Copyright ©2014 Brandy Walker

Cover by Brandy Walker

Edited by Noel Varner

ISBN-10: 0692232958
ISBN-13: 978-0692232958

All Rights Are Reserved. No part of this book may be used or reproduced in any manner whatsoever without written permission, except in the case of brief quotations embodied in critical articles and reviews.

First Print Publication June 2014

This book is a work of fiction. The names, characters, places, and incidents are products of the writer's imagination or have been used fictitiously and are not to be construed as real. Any resemblance to persons, living or dead, actual events, locale or organizations is entirely coincidental.

Dedication:

For my husband Todd.
Without you by my side I would be drifting through the air with no idea what to do. Love you to pieces!

Acknowledgments:

I couldn't do this without the help of Roz and Sheri. Your feedback pushed me to make this a better book. I also couldn't have gotten everything just right without the help of my editor Noel.

Thank you to my family for being supportive in this adventure. I love being able to celebrate it with all of you.

Prologue

HIGH SCHOOL 10 YEARS AGO...

Sitting high up in the bleachers Laurel Kane leaned back and lowered the camera to her lap. Sighing in delight, she watched the football team finish practice for the day. Players milled about looking exhausted and excited for the game the next night. A few were gathered around the coach for last minute instructions, while others hovered around the coolers pulling down long drinks of water before ripping off their jerseys and pads and heading back to the locker room. All of that male teenage muscle, sweaty and rippling, caused her to blush.

Looking through the viewfinder again, Laurel scanned the boys looking for the one that tripped her heart at every turn. She didn't find him near the coach or water cooler, but had a good idea where he might be. Moving her gaze to the gaggle of girls on the sidelines, she finally saw him. Quinton Ferris. Jersey and pads flung over his broad shoulder and Marcy Pitt grinning up at him like a buffoon.

Figures. Marcy was your typical bubbly, big-breasted blond, head of the cheerleading squad, Homecoming Queen and all around Princess of the school. Of course she would be all over Quin. He was hot, dangerous and so popular Laurel was sure even the outcasts of the school liked him. Every guy wanted to be him and every girl wanted to date him. The only exceptions to the general rule were his younger brothers Revlin and Kegen; twins who were a year younger than Quin and their own force to be reckoned with.

Ignoring the voice in her head telling her not to do it, she snapped a few pictures of Quin's hot body before standing and making her way down the steps. She wanted to get back to the yearbook room and select the candid pictures for the six-page football section that still needed to be finished.

Reaching the bottom of the stairs, Laurel cast one last glance in Quin's direction. Lifting the camera she snapped one more picture right as he turned her way, staring at her with his intense dark brown eyes. His dark hair fell across his forehead and a knowing smirk graced his lips "Hope you got a good one of me for the yearbook, *Camera Girl*. Or was that for your personal collection? I heard you have a pretty extensive one of me." Quin laughed, slinging his free arm over Marcy's shoulders, the other girls surrounding him giggled and snickered along with him.

Laurel stiffened, the blood draining from her face before being replaced by the heat of embarrassment. She dropped the camera to hang around her neck, took one last look at Quin as her heart broke, and then spun away. She forced back the desire to run but couldn't resist picking up her pace, walking as fast as she could without making a bigger fool of herself. She felt fat tears roll down her face and over her hot cheeks. It was silly to cry over what he'd said, but she couldn't help it. The first time he'd said anything to her, ever really looked at her, and it had been to get a laugh at her expense.

A bit on the shy and nerdy side, Laurel had only a few friends and even less confidence. She liked to view the world from behind the lens of a camera where it was safe. She preferred to observe and capture defining moments on film. Interacting with people never really paid off in her experience.

Resisting the urge to look back, Laurel made it to the classroom near the field, never noticing Quin's too aware gaze following her progress. She never saw the flash of regret that crossed his face as she slammed the door closed behind her.

Chapter One

The group of skydivers Laurel was with finally touched ground and her job for the day, for the assignment, was over. The jumpers walking toward her were brimming with excitement, as they should be. Today had been a big day for them all.

Lowering her camera, Laurel was overcome with a sudden sense of déjà vu as she scanned the group coming toward her. Standing out in the pack, just like he always had, was Quinton Ferris. A tall, thin woman with long blond hair was chatting a mile a minute next to him and grinning like an idiot. Seemed some things never changed.

Imagine her surprise the first time she came out with her friends and found the Ferris brothers, bigger and badder than ever. Of all the things in the world they could have done, they decided to open a skydiving business, a fairly successful one too. Not that she would ever admit to scouring the Internet to find out every last detail she could about them though. She spent a large amount of that time convincing herself it was purely research for the book she was putting together for one of the publishers she did freelance work for.

Raising the camera again, Laurel took a couple more candid shots before turning it off and setting it behind her on the picnic table. She hopped up on the tabletop, thankful to finally rest for a couple of minutes. She knew she had plenty of photos, and it was time to start sifting through them all. Before she could do that, however, she needed to load the SUV and endure the hour drive home.

The most random thought popped into her head as she gathered the stuff around her. *God, I hope all of the pictures aren't just of Quin like in high school.*

Even after that dreadful day in school, she still couldn't tear her eyes from him or stop her heart from beating out of control when he was near. She had endured weeks of teasing and humiliation as every girl that ever had a crush on him used Laurel's pain to feel better. They, at least, hadn't been made fun of from the object of their affection.

Those damn cheerleaders spread it around the entire school that *Camera Girl,* or *Lovesick Laurel* was taking pictures of Quin and plastering them all over her bedroom. They even started a rumor about seeing her kissing and talking to a picture of him like he was her boyfriend.

As if I would ever have done that in public. Privately…when locked away in my room with no one around to hear…sure. I'll admit to that.

Not once did Quin say he was sorry for ruining her life. He passed her in the hall without a glance, never a sign of guilt or regret. She went back to the 'never existed' category where he was concerned and, in a way, she was glad for it. At least that's what she tried to convince herself was true. Secretly she had been crushed. Her heart broken even though she knew, in reality, they would never be boyfriend and girlfriend. She wasn't that delusional.

"Earth to Laurel. Where the hell are you?" A voice slowly broke into her thoughts.

Blinking rapidly, Laurel looked up into Sean Crutchfield's twinkling eyes. "Hey Sean. Great jump. You guys looked fantastic up there."

"You think so? Did you get all of the pictures you needed? We can probably go up again. Maybe try a formation or something." Sean grinned. The excitement of what he had just done pouring off him.

"Hey numb-nuts, if you didn't notice, Laurel put the camera away." Monica sashayed up, wrapping her arm around Sean's waist.

Sean looked down at his girlfriend. "Numb-nuts? No, I think they're okay. Wanna check 'em for me?" Sean winked as Monica punched him in the arm.

Laurel laughed at her friends' antics. It was never a dull moment with them around. The rest of the group slowly joined them: Teri and Rick, Denise and Keith, and her cousin Jason heading up the rear with the instructors. Sliding her sunglasses on, Laurel watched as Quin, Blondie and Quin's younger brother, she thought it was Kegen, walked past uttering great jump before heading inside the hanger.

With a sigh she stood, stretched her back out, then began gathering up her gear again. Her friends were staying for the celebration barbecue the Chute Shack crew was throwing in honor of the group earning their C licenses. They had all completed 200 jumps, finished their written and oral exams, and could now do open field demos and certain high altitude jumps. For as much time and energy as they all put into it, the celebration was definitely deserved. Unfortunately, she needed to get going so she could make some progress on the book. It certainly wasn't going to pick out the right pictures and get the layouts and wording done on its own.

"Okay guys, I'm out."

The group protested but she wouldn't be swayed.

"You know I need to get to work. The deadline is coming up and I knew with your jump schedule I'd be cutting it close. I have to get this done. I'll be starting my next assignment this coming week."

Monica, the honorary mom of the group, spoke up. "Come on Laurel, can't you stay for a little bit? Just a couple of hours—long enough for a burger or dog. Maybe you could get some pictures of the after party? You know, to wrap up the book."

"I wish I could, but it's a long drive home and I have at least five hours of work ahead of me. I haven't even looked through the six hundred pictures I took today. Add that to the eight hundred from the previous two days and well....you get the idea. I'm thinking an all-nighter is in order."

"Damn Laurel, think you got enough? You might want to take a few more just in case." Jason chuckled as he gave her a quick hug and kiss on the head.

"Ha, ha! It's better to have too many than not enough."

"That's what you always say. Give me a few minutes and I'll help load your gear. I need to get out of this harness real quick."

Jason jogged off, the rest of the group following him after saying quick goodbyes. 1

She was digging in her purse for her keys when a noise drew her attention to the hanger everyone had disappeared into. She was startled to find Quin staring back at her from a distance. His arms were crossed over his broad chest, head tilted slightly to one side, and a contemplative look etched across his features.

***

Quin stood right inside the hanger waiting for the group to come in. They were saying goodbye to the photographer. There was something familiar about her that tugged at him, like he had met her before but didn't know where. He snatched at a memory that flickered to life, but it vanished as quickly as it had appeared.

Jason, the guy who coordinated the group's training, sprinted into the hanger, slipped out of his harness and jogged back out to her as the rest of the group straggled in.

Quin couldn't help but watch as Jason and the woman chatted while gathering up her gear and disappearing around the corner of the building with her. Seconds later he was walking back.

"You get your girl off okay?" Quin asked as soon as Jason was in earshot.

"Yeah, she's got work to do and couldn't hang out. Thanks for letting her photograph everything. I know the book is going to be great once she gets it done. It has a pretty quick turnaround and, once she's done, it shouldn't take too long to get into production. That should be great for you guys."

Quin shrugged, "Rev said we would be mentioned in it so there wasn't much to lose. And you're right, the publicity will be great." Quin was all about having the business get more publicity, especially with the next Boogie they were currently scheduling. The skydiving event was going to be the largest they ever held. Four days long with multiple Skydiving teams, various aircrafts, demos and more. It was going to be one giant skydiving party and would put them well above the other businesses in the area. If the book brought more buzz to the Chute Shack, then who was he to complain?

Quin followed Jason inside to see his crew pulling beers out of the fridge and rolling the barbecue grill out back. Jason sauntered over to Sami, flashing a million-watt smile. He guessed that with his girlfriend gone, Jason could play like he wanted. *What a prick.*

Quin might be a serial dater but he never two-timed a woman. Having it happen to him with someone he thought he loved had quickly solidified his stance on the whole thing. If something wasn't working, he cut ties and moved on. There wasn't a woman around who complained about his honesty when it came to relationships. The ones who didn't like it moved on pretty fast, the others were content to let it die a natural death. He had yet to find the woman that would make him want to give her his forever.

Watching Jason with Sami, Quin became more and more annoyed. Jason moved forward into her personal space, brushing against her chest, then trailed his fingers down her back. He could see a shiver run through her from where he stood. Quin personally knew how Sami reacted when she was attracted and turned on. They'd spent five years together on and off before they both decided they made better friends than lovers.

Just because they both craved extreme sports, didn't mean they were meant to be together. When they were alone and not having sex, they were fighting or just completely ignoring each other. Granted, the fighting led to great make up sex but in the end it didn't make for a lasting relationship.

It looked to him that Jason and his friends were just using the girlfriend to get published in a book. Quin frowned and shook his head. The irritation crawling over his skin surprised him. It shouldn't bother him this much that the woman was being cheated on. It wasn't like he had a stake in the relationship with her. Some people just had no shame.

"What's up with you big brother?" A glance over his shoulder he saw his younger brother Rev approaching him from behind. The big brother comment always made him laugh. Rev was just as big as he was and really not that much younger. Soon after he was born his mom became pregnant with Revlin and Kegen. They were Irish Twins, well Irish Triplets but not in the traditional sense, there were three babies all born in the same year. He wasn't sure how his parents coped with it all then or now. They might be grown but he imagined their parents still thought they were a handful.

"Nothing's up. Just taking it all in."

"If it's nothing, why are you giving J-Man the evil eye? You upset he's hitting on Sami?"

They both looked in Sami and Jason's direction. Jason was leaning over whispering into her ear. His right hand that earlier had trailed down her back, was now cupped firmly over her backside. Quin probed how he felt about it and came up with nothing. He didn't feel any hints of jealousy, only irritation that the guy was cheating on his photographer girlfriend, or at least headed down that path.

"No, not mad that he's hitting on her. We've been over for a while now, but he does have a girlfriend. You know how I feel about cheaters."

"Yeah, I do know how you feel but he doesn't have a girlfriend." Rev looked confused, which in turn made Quin stop and think. Hadn't anyone else noticed the brunette sitting at the picnic table taking pictures? Or when she was standing in the middle of the drop zone as they came down? It was all he could do to avoid landing on top of her when she suddenly moved into his landing spot. She had been completely oblivious to her surroundings and damn near got them both hurt.

"Didn't you see the woman taking pictures? His girlfriend?"

Rev chuckled and popped him on the back. "That's not his girlfriend bro, so there's no need to get your panties in a wad and tick off one of our best customers. They're talking about staying with us to get their D license. It wouldn't hurt business to have a few more USPA instructors coming out of our place."

"No shit? I just assumed when he was all over the photographer that they were together. He came in here and started flirting with Sami so my mind took off."

"You are pretty good at jumping to conclusions. If you'd taken the time to actually get to know the group, and not hole yourself up in the office half the time, you'd have learned that Jason and Laurel are cousins. Laurel is a freelance photographer and when she got the look-book assignment Jason suggested she do it here since he was planning the jump weekend for his group."

"Huh, well I *almost* feel like an ass. At least I didn't confront him on it." Quin shook his head to clear it of the uncalled for anger. It wasn't like him to get butt-hurt over a woman like that. "Come on, let's grab some grub. Looks like Kegen is about done grilling."

As they walked toward their brother, Quin glanced over his shoulder at Rev. "Hey, did the chick seem familiar to you?"

"The chick? You mean Laurel, the camera girl? Not really. But then, I didn't pay that much attention to her. Was concentrating more on the clients and the job. Why?"

"No reason. Just thought there was something familiar about her. Couldn't pin-point what though."

"She isn't one of your random exes is she?"

"No. I would have remembered her. She's not an *ex* but definitely someone I knew once, I'm sure of it." Now if he could remember how he knew her maybe he wouldn't have this nagging thought that he'd messed up already.

Chapter Two

It took Laurel longer to get home than she expected. A big accident on the highway had her stewing in her SUV for an hour while traffic inched along. By the time she pulled into her driveway, she was ready to cry with relief.

Opening the door to her little two-bedroom cottage, she dropped everything but her camera bag just inside the door, slamming it shut and locking it.

Eager to download the last set of images and start working, she made her way down the hall to the spare room that doubled as an office. Maneuvering through the darkened room, she hit the enter key on the keyboard lighting the room with the monitor's glow. Pulling one of the SD cards out of the bag she slid it into the slot, the soft grinding noise from the computer letting her know it was pulling up her photo program.

Knowing it would take a couple of minutes for everything to load, Laurel made her way to her bedroom and grabbed the sweats and tank off the bed where she'd thrown them that morning. It had been a long day out in the sun, and it was absolutely time to get cleaned up and comfy.

She didn't doubt the words she'd spoken earlier. An all-nighter was definitely on tap. It was her routine no matter how long she had been awake, loving the design portion of her job almost as much as the photography.

Moving through the house flipping on lights on the way to the kitchen, she went over everything she had mapped out in her head. There were a couple of ideas that would have to be tanked since she didn't have the nerve to ask to go up on one of the flights. Hopefully, she would have plenty of other great images to fill that void.

The more she thought about the missing shots, the more it bothered her. She really should have gotten on the plane while it was on the ground…at the very least. When she first received the assignment, the publisher sent a list of suggested images ranging from the empty interior of the aircraft up to the jumpers exiting the plane. The idea of actually stepping foot on the plane, even while it was on the ground, sent terror through her veins.

After rummaging through the pantry and coming up with a couple of granola bars, she opened the fridge and, mid-grab of a bottle of water, had a brilliant thought. She could just ask Jason to do it. Nothing like solving a problem after the fact. Plucking out the water bottle she dashed to the front door where she had left her bags.

He should have no problem popping out to the Chute Shack and asking Revlin to help him out since they seemed to be good friends. He could even do it on his next jump; too bad she didn't know when that was. It would need to be soon, though, so she could finish the project by the deadline.

Excited about getting what she needed, she grabbed up her purse and dug through it to find her cell phone. Hitting Jason's number she was connected in seconds, listening to the ring echo over and over before his voicemail kicked in. Leaving a quick message she shuffled back to her office. Hopefully he would get back to her tonight, unless of course, a woman preoccupied him. If that were the case, she wouldn't hear back from him for a while.

Laurel set her water and snacks on the desk before sliding into her office chair. The chill from the leather seat seeped through her sweat pants into the backs of her tired legs, sending a shiver through her. Leaning over she snatched up the cardigan left on the futon, putting it on before starting the long task of sifting through the images. The pictures were sorted into the *yes* or *no* folders with quite a few ending up in the *filler* pile. A couple of hours drifted by and it wasn't until she was out of water and needed a bathroom break that she tried Jason again. With no answer still, it finally hit her that he probably didn't have his cell on him, as usual, so the best way to get hold of him would be to call the Chute Shack. They would still be there if they were partying, maybe.

The momentary thought of Quin answering the phone sent butterflies skyrocketing through her belly. It *was* his place of business. It would make sense if he answered—she tried to convince herself. She wasn't that same shy girl from years ago. She could hold a conversation with a man, with *him*, without sounding like a fool.

Drawing in a quick breath she found the number and dialed, her desire to talk to Jason outweighing the possibility of Quin answering the phone. Hell, Revlin or Kegen could just as easily pick up.

Disappointment sprang to life as the phone continued to ring in her ear with no answer. Hanging up, she waited a couple of minutes debating whether or not to call back, indecision and anxiety over getting those needed images warring for dominance.

"Maybe they couldn't hear it with the party going on."

It might be useless, but she needed to talk to Jason about another jump. The overwhelming urgency of the situation ate at her. At this point she would go out there and do it. Who cared if the thought of going up in a tiny plane scared the pants off her? She needed those pictures.

Decision made, she redialed with the same result. She was about to hang up when someone finally picked up.

"The Chute Shack," a deep, smooth masculine voice rumbled through the line.

She wasn't sure whom the voice on the line belonged to and it didn't matter, at least to her body. Shivers worked their way down her spine as goosebumps popped up on her arms. Fuck—that was a potent voice. She hadn't spent much time talking to any of the brothers or their crew, and she wished to hell she had. At least she knew it didn't belong to any of the women working there and she wasn't getting turned on by them, not that knowing that fact eased her anxiety any.

"Hello?"

"Oh! I'm looking for Jason Owens. He was there earlier with the group that got their C licenses."

"Sorry, they all left a little bit ago. It is rolling onto midnight and we're about to head out ourselves."

"Oh my gosh! I'm so sorry. I didn't even think to look at the time. I just got this idea in my head, and I needed to talk to him about another jump. Damn, I wish I would have said something to him earlier when I was there."

"Is this, um, uh, the camera girl, Laurel?"

Laurel's heart stalled in her chest. As quickly as it stopped, it started up again—going right past normal and into holy shit racing speed. *It's him! He sounds just like he did when he called me that all those years ago.*

She did her best to pull it together. Hoping her voice didn't betray the astonishment she felt at hearing those words from Quin again. "Quin Ferris? Damn. I haven't been called *Camera Girl* since high school."

***

Quin was stunned into silence. Hearing Laurel's voice on the other end of the phone was a surprise, but not as big as the surprise hearing her words brought.

In a flash he made the connection between the woman with the camera today and the shy girl in high school that took pictures for the yearbook. He also remembered how he'd embarrassed her back then by joking about her taking pictures of him for her personal collection.

At the oddest times during the past ten years he would recall that moment. The flash of pain that crossed her face, the red flush of embarrassment rushing to her cheeks, then the tears he wasn't sure she was aware of trickling down. He regretted his words the minute they left his mouth, but he was full of boyish pride and surrounded by girls who fawned all over him. They made him feel like he was the king of the world, better than everyone else when in reality he wasn't. His mother had taught him better than to think with his ego.

It wasn't until later that he found out how much his words carried weight in their tiny world. His girlfriend at the time bragged about how she and her friends teased *Camera Girl* every chance they got. They even came up with a name on their own, *Lovesick Laurel*. She said people like her needed to be reminded where their place in life was. That they could only ever look at the beautiful and popular and should never be allowed to think they could rise up out of their place in society.

Every time he saw *Camera Girl* after that he was so ashamed that he'd unknowingly made her life a living hell. He couldn't look at or even acknowledge she existed. Hit by the shock of learning who Laurel was, Quin turned to lean against his desk. His body felt shaky and nervous and he needed some solid wood to hold him upright.

Her soft voice coming through the line pulled him from his memories. "Hello, Quin? Are you still there?"

"Yeah, I'm still here. How did you know it was me and not Rev or Kegen?" It was a silly thing to ask, but he was still trying to pull himself together.

"You're the one who got everyone calling me *Camera Girl*. I don't think I'll ever forget that."

He started to say something but she interrupted.

"I'm sorry to keep you later than you planned. I'll just try Jason on his cell again. Well, maybe tomorrow. I'm sure it can wait. I hope you have a good night."

Laurel's sweet voice was clipped and professional sounding, and he found he didn't like that. He could tell she wanted to get off the phone, but he wanted to keep her on the line a little longer. Maybe get forgiveness from her for his actions in the past. He didn't like her thinking of him as a juvenile ass. Not that she said he had been, but he knew that's what he had been. There was a burning need for him to give her a better memory of him, hell of them together.

"Wait! You said something about a jump. Is there something I can help you with?"

She hesitated on the other end. He held his breath, hoping she wouldn't hang up. When he didn't hear the call disconnect, he continued on.

"Are you interested in jumping? I'd be happy to book you for a jump with me if you are. And, just so you know, that isn't something Jason can help you with. He isn't qualified for that."

"Oh no! I could never jump out of an airplane. It's for the book. I just wanted to know if he had another jump coming up."

Damn. There went the fleeting thought of doing a tandem with her strapped to the front of him. Of having her tight little body pressed up against his as they sat in the plane waiting to get to the drop zone. He may not have talked to her, but he sure as hell noticed her when she was at the Shack. Her brown hair was typically pulled back into a ponytail. Her face free of make-up and each time he had seen her she sported a tank top that molded to her high, perky breasts and cargo pants that hugged her trim ass. She looked sexy in a completely understated way. Reaching down he adjusted his fly, as thoughts of running his hands over her curves raced through his mind. He cleared his throat and got back on topic. "No. They didn't book anything when they left. He said he'd call when they figured out their next step."

"Damn! There goes that plan."

He couldn't help the chuckle that came out at her vehement exclamation.

"I guess I'll just have to seriously think about plan B. I really don't want to, really wanted to avoid it, but I guess I can't."

He couldn't say for sure, but it didn't sound like she was even talking to him, more like she was mumbling to herself.

"Laurel?"

"Hmmm?"

The dreamy quality of her voice made his cock twitch again. "Is there something I can help you with? Did you not get a shot of something you needed?"

He wouldn't mind getting an up close and personal look at her. All evening while everyone partied, Quin found his thoughts drifting back to the quiet woman. He spent little to no time with her when she was out on the drop zone, something he was sorry for now. Plus, ever since it hit him a couple of minutes ago who she was, he felt an overwhelming need to fix things between them. He just needed to see her again. It had to be in person though. This wasn't something he wanted to do over the phone. He wanted her to see he was sincere.

"Yes and no." She hesitated again before continuing on. "It isn't a required shot, just something that would make the book that much better. The publisher suggested shots of the interior of the plane and some of the people when they jumped out, but I didn't have the nerve to ask. To be honest, the thought of getting in one of those tiny planes, let's just say I find small places confining."

So that's why she was so adamant about not jumping from a plane.

Quin's brain went into overdrive. What the hell could he do to get her back out there so he could spend time with her, feel things out? It needed to be something that was all business with the possibility of one-on-one time.

He glanced around his office, his gaze landing on the calendar. "Perfect!"

"What? I don't think…"

He interrupted her before she went further. "No. It's not perfect that you're claustrophobic."

"Hey now! I didn't say I was claustrophobic. I just don't like small, confined spaces where there is a possibility of lots of people."

Quin chuckled. This woman was a lot different than the girl in high school, and he was starting to really like her. "Now honey, don't get bent out of shape. It's fine. We can work on that too if you want. I'm sure I can help you love tight, close quarters when it's just you and me. We could have the entire plane to do whatever we wanted."

A small, soft gasp made its way through the phone line. His voice must have dipped at the end making his arousal apparent as he thought about everything he wanted to do to her if he got her alone on the aircraft. First on the list was joining the mile high club. He knew he could get her to make that sound again when he pushed his cock inside her willing body.

Adjusting himself again he turned to sit in his chair, his painfully hard erection pressing against the zipper of his jeans. He tried shaking his airplane fantasies away but only managed to replace them with ones involving his office.

He could envision bending her over his desk and taking her hard from behind. She would have to stretch to wrap her hands around the front edge of the desk, lifting her ass a little higher to get just the right grip.

A groan slipped from his lips before he could stop it. Clearing his throat, he tried to cover it up.

"As I was saying, I have the perfect solution for your problem. I'm an aerial photographer and can get the shots you want. We've got Friday Freefall coming up. We can do it then."

"What's Friday Freefall?"

"Every other week on Fridays, the crew takes the day to work on freestyle maneuvers. The choreographed maneuvers we do for shows, demos and competitions."

"And you think you can get the pictures I want? That could work. It's definitely better than the idea I came up with. Do you want me to email a list of the things I'm looking for?

Oh no, she isn't getting out of this that easy. "No. I think it would be better for you to be here."

"I don't know. I'm sure a list would be fine. You can get other pictures you think would be good too, I'll trust your judgment since I've never been in the air like that. You can send them to me and I'll go through them. I'll make sure you get photography credit too."

"No. It's best if you're here with me so we can go through them together. I want to make sure I don't miss anything. Besides, you can bring your camera and get pictures from the ground of the stunts and maneuvers. Might make a great addition to the book."

"It would be nice to get a few more shots in. What time do you want me there?"

Score! "Let's see, I'll be here around five. So you should be too."

"P.M.?"

"No sweetheart, five in the morning."

"You've got to be joking. It takes me an hour to get out there. Are you sure I need to be there that early?"

"A lot goes on before we head up. Think of it this way, you'll get the fly on the wall view of what goes on behind the scenes. You didn't see that part before."

"Ugh! I'm warning you now. I am *not* a morning person, but I really want those pictures, so you're on."

"Great, I'll see you this Friday." Quin glanced at his watch. "I need to get going, its pretty late and I have an early morning."

"I hate to break it to you, but it's morning already. I'm sorry—again—for keeping you later than you planned. I guess I should head to bed too. Start storing up the sleep I'm bound to lose waking up so early Friday."

"Night Laurel. Hope you sleep well."

"Night. Oh, and Quin?"

"Yeah?"

"Thank you."

The softly spoken words caressed his ears long after she hung up.

Chapter Three

Thursday rolled around a lot quicker than Laurel thought it would.

During the week she worked on the layout of the book, narrowing down the images she wanted included and talking to the publisher about the extra photos she would be getting. She began research on her next assignment at the upcoming wedding expo. Finally, she got hold of Jason and got to hear all about his hookup with Sami, the leggy blond from the Chute Shack. Not that she asked to know the details, but Jason had a tendency to over share.

Laurel wasn't too surprised to hear that Quin and Sami had been an item for years, and that only recently did they decide to break up for good. She had to squash the tiny leap of joy in her heart upon hearing that bit of news. She thought he may have made a sexual innuendo over the phone, but was sure if he did, it was something he didn't even think about. It was probably as natural to him as walking or breathing.

What really surprised Laurel was how easy it was to talk to Quin on the phone after they got beyond the slow start. She only experienced a few minutes of panic when he basically demanded she come out for the jump and go over the pictures with him in person. She would have been fine letting him send her everything and sifting through it all after the fact. Actually, she probably would have been happier doing it that way, content to work on other projects and keep her mind off of him. Instead, she spent her days looking at too many pictures that included Quin, which led to her falling asleep with him fresh in her memory.

Hopefully, when she showed up Friday morning, none of those nightly dreams would show on her face and she would be able to talk to him as easily in person as she had on the phone. All without blushing or nervously biting her lip.

She was still getting used to her renewed awareness of Quin. In her mind, he was the one who got away. The guy who drifted into her thoughts, as she wondered what he was up to throughout the years.

It was best to focus on what she knew was going to happen. Quin was going to take aerial photos, they were going to go over them to make sure nothing was missed, and then she would say thank you and goodbye. That was it. Nothing. More!

Packing the rest of her gear, she lined the bags up by the front door next to the cooler of snacks she'd packed earlier. She was ready to go and desperately needed to head to bed, even if it was a bit early for her. Three-thirty came awfully early in the morning, and no matter how excited she was about completing the project…that was a horrible time to get up!

Flipping the light off in her room, she eased beneath the cool covers on her bed. As soon as her head hit the pillow and she closed her eyes, images of Quin filled her mind. She was no longer surprised when it happened. She let the fantasy of him slowly making his way down her body drag her under into sweet oblivion.

Overly loud music yanked Laurel from her dreams. Quin was just about to bring her to orgasm when she jolted upright. Clutching her hand to her chest, she tried to steady her breathing.

"Fuck, right when I was about to climax!"

She flopped back and waited for her heart to stop racing before rolling out of bed. Stumbling to the bathroom, she got ready for what was bound to be a long, hot day. A day that started too damn early for her.

Thirty minutes later, a piece of peanut butter toast was consumed; a cup of coffee downed, a thermos of coffee brewed and the car packed. All that was left to do was lock up and head out.

Butterflies took flight in her stomach the minute she sat behind the wheel of the SUV. The thought of seeing Quin so soon after he rolled out of bed and knowing she would be working with him all day made her light-headed and giddy. She'd never spent any real time with him when she'd been on the drop zone before. The one and only encounter they had was when he almost landed on her. She was so out of it, concentrating on getting shots of everyone as they landed, she didn't even realize she was in danger of being landed on.

At the last minute he was able steer clear of her, landing a few feet away. He told her to watch it as he walked past her, irritation clearly written all over his face. After that, she made an effort to stay far away from him and the other jumpers on his crew.

She spent the entire drive out to the Chute Shack going over the shots she wanted, prepping what she was going to say to him, and convincing herself to keep it professional and not let on that the only jumping she wanted to do involved him being naked and willing.

Pulling into the parking lot at five o'clock on the dot, she parked next to one of the huge black and gray trucks bearing the Chute Shack logo. At least she knew someone was here.

Hopping out of the SUV, she snatched her thermos up before grabbing her gear bags and cooler from the back. Making her way to the front door, she was sidelined by one of the twins before she could even knock.

"Hey Laurel. Front door is still locked. Come around this way."

Revlin or Kegen, she really wasn't sure which one, held open the chain-link gate door the employees usually used.

"Thanks. Um…"

A slight grin tipped the corner of his mouth. He took the gear bags from her and motioned for her to go through ahead of him. "Revlin."

The heat of a blush climbed up her cheeks with the knowledge that he knew she didn't know which twin he was. "Thanks Revlin."

"Please call me Rev. Only my mom called me Revlin and, sweetheart, you don't look anything like her." He gave her a once over as she moved in front of him. "I have to admit, I was a little surprised when Quin said you'd be coming out here today. I thought you were done with the pictures."

"I thought I was too but there are a few shots I didn't get that I really want. Quin offered to get them for me and insisted I come out so we can preview them together in case something got missed."

"That's cool. You couldn't have picked a better aerial photographer than Quin. He's really mastered all of the ins and outs of it."

"So not everyone does the videos and pictures?" She assumed all skydivers did actually. With all of the new camera systems out, it had to make things a lot easier. She really should have known better than to assume. Anyone could pick up a camera and take a picture, but not everyone could capture a moment and have emotion shine through.

Rev chuckled behind her. "Hell no. It takes a lot of time to become a skydiver and even more to learn the photography portion of it. You have to really multi-task and master getting just the right shots. You can't be too far in front, above or below. Not to mention making sure you don't run into anyone when they're doing aerial maneuvers. You can't really use your hands either. You need those to keep stable while flying through the air."

"Wow. I didn't know. There's a lot more that goes into it than I ever thought. It's pretty impressive he can do it all."

"What's impressive, honey?" Quin's deep voice had her stopping on a dime, causing Rev to plow into her.

Quin jumped forward, catching her before she went face first in the dirt. He wrapped his arms around her waist, pulling her close. Her breath caught in her throat as her eyes travelled from his bare chest and up his throat before landing on his lips. Lips she spent many a night dreaming about. Without thought, she licked her own. The groan vibrating through Quin pulled her gaze up to his face, snagging on the look of desire in his eyes.

Rev cleared his throat behind her. "I'll just take these inside."

Laurel barely noticed when Rev slipped the cooler and thermos of coffee from her hands, too caught up in being engulfed in Quin's strong arms. Her nipples beaded, poking at the thin cotton of her bra. No doubt showing through her shirt as well.

She never imagined she would be in this position, dreamed about it yes, but never thought she would be up close and personal with Quinton Ferris. It was a high school fantasy come true. The teenage girl in her was hoping things would go a little further, maybe a kiss. The adult in her was telling her to keep it professional.

"You okay, honey?"

"Hmm?"

Quin chuckled. "Are you okay from when Rev rammed into you pitching you forward?"

Laurel nodded her head and urged her body to move out of his arms, but it just didn't happen. "I'm fine. It was my fault anyway for stopping in front of him like that. I hope I didn't hurt him."

"I'm sure he's fine. Running into you will probably be the highlight of his day and will be nothing compared to slamming into the ground if and when he lands wrong. He seems to fly a little freer at times. He and Kegen like to hot dog it up there a bit too much on days like this."

"Oh, if you say so." As much as she wanted to stay in the warmth and comfort of his arms, it wasn't appropriate; especially after giving herself the '*keep it professional*' talk. "You can let go of me now Quin. I promise I won't fall."

He sighed like he really wasn't interested in letting go, but did anyway.

Laurel pushed her hair behind her ear. "Thanks for catching me."

Quin grinned at her and it did a funny thing to her heart. "Anytime, Laurel."

She cleared her throat and lost her will to keep eye contact, she looked around before her gaze landed back on his bare chest.

"Do you always run around without a shirt on, or was that just for my benefit? I would think it is a bit early and chilly to be stripping down."

Quin laughed as he rubbed a hand down his chest. She was riveted to the movement, tracking its progress over the taut, smooth skin. She sucked in a breath and forced her focus back to his face.

"No. I generally have clothes on. Kegen managed to spill his coffee on me this morning. I was in the middle of finding a shirt when I heard you pull up. That's why Rev went out to get you instead of me. I was just wondering what was taking him so long to bring you back here."

Quin grabbed her hand up, lacing his fingers with hers. She wasn't quite sure what made him do it and any minute she would protest and pull her hand away, which she didn't. Next she knew they were locked away from his brothers in his office. He pushed her down into an office chair before he took another.

"So, let's talk about the photos you want."

"Um, Quin? Don't you want to put on a shirt?" Not that she wanted him to cover up but if she wanted to get her mind back on the job, then he needed to be clothed. All that tan flesh was tempting her to lean forward and take a lick. Or better yet, a bite.

"Huh." He looked down at his chest then back at her. "Am I distracting you?" The cheeky grin on his face was enough to make her roll her eyes.

"No, not a distraction," she lied. "But I'd hate for you to catch a cold or something while sitting around here half naked."

"Don't you like my half naked state, honey?"

Laurel's mouth dropped. If he only knew what thoughts were going through her head. She'd like him fully naked and served up for her to eat. Licking her lips again, she let her gaze travel over Quin's hard body. The things she wanted to do to him. He must have gotten a clue to her thoughts, turning away suddenly to grab a shirt off the bookshelf behind him.

Laurel averted her eyes, embarrassed by her brazen move and made a determined search for a pen. Finding one next to the computer, she snatched it up along with a pad of paper.

Without raising her head she addressed him. "So, here's what I was thinking for the photos."

***

Quin glanced down, pinpointing his landing spot once again. He didn't plan on it when he exited the plane and shot the last of the images of his brothers, but seeing Laurel standing on the drop zone glowing with happiness, he made his decision. He was going to land as close to her as possible and finally get that kiss he was aching for.

All day long he worked side-by-side with her looking over the images in his office, discussing what else she should have, and just getting to know her. The need to constantly touch her anytime she was near just about drove him nuts. He found himself sitting closer, brushing against her arm or leg. He even plucked imaginary lint off her shirt one time just to keep her with him a few seconds more.

The longer he spent with her, the more he found he wanted her. Preferably naked and underneath him but, at this point, he'd take what he could get.

She was funny, witty, and nowhere close to being that painfully shy girl from high school. She had turned into a beautiful, self-confident woman who had a passion for photography that lit her up from the inside.

She laughed at his brothers' ridiculous jokes. Cleaned and bandaged his pilot JD's finger when he cut it on a knife while fixing lunch. And pretty much bonded with everyone in the Shack. She fit in without trying, something that was hard to do if you weren't part of the group.

Sure they were friendly with their customers, but she was different. He didn't know how much he wanted her to fit in until he realized she already did.

Touching ground ten feet away from Laurel; he whipped off his helmet while striding toward her, the parachute dragging behind him. Once he got up close he saw the surprise on her face. Not wanting to give her too long to protest, he cupped the side of her face with one hand, caressing her cheek with his thumb, then dove in for a kiss.

The second his mouth touched hers, he was lost. The soft, silkiness beneath his lips lured him to increase the pressure. When she didn't respond, he instantly panicked and started to pull away. It never crossed his mind that she wasn't feeling the same need and pull as him.

Before he broke contact completely, Laurel's hands slid up his chest, leaving a wake of heat on their journey over his body. She wrapped her arms around his neck, fingers delving into his hair. The tight grasp sent shards of arousal through him. Grabbing her around the waist he hauled her against him, his erection grinding against her soft belly.

What started out as a gentle teasing of the lips turned into full on passion. He nipped her lower lip before driving inside the moist heat of her mouth when she gasped.

A low snicker and a couple of cat-calls invaded his brain.

Laurel pulled back before dropping her head and looking everywhere but at him. He didn't miss the blush painting her cheeks. Spinning away she started making her way back to the hanger.

Quin looked around to see who interrupted what had to be the best kiss he ever had the pleasure of taking part in.

Rev stood next to them. "Yo' bro, we need to get in. Looks like a storm is rolling in. I would hate for the equipment to get ruined." He pointed down to the helmet, the two cameras still attached and vulnerable to the elements. Granted, they jumped in weather before; but if he could avoid getting gear wet, he would.

"Yeah," he grunted. Jogging to catch up to Laurel he placed his hand in hers, neither said a word. He chanced a glance at her and saw she was nibbling on her bottom lip.

Damn that was going to drive him nuts. "What's going on in that mind of yours, honey?"

She let go of her lip and graced him with a small smile. "Just wondering what that was about."

"What? Rev interrupting or…?"

She bumped him with her shoulder. "The kiss," she said softly. "You know I almost decided it was a bad idea."

"You had to know I've been dying to kiss you all day and, from the way you kissed me back, I'd say you felt the same way."

She chuckled softly and lightly squeezed his hand. "I've wanted to kiss you since high school."

"That's a long ass time. Did it live up to your expectations?"

"If you couldn't decipher my reaction, then maybe we shouldn't do it again. I'm still trying to figure out what you're up to anyway, so maybe not kissing again *is* a good idea."

"First off, I think you enjoyed me kissing you. Second, we will be kissing again. A lot. And third, I'm not up to anything, honey. I like you and I want to get to know you better."

"How do you want to get to know me better? By kissing me senseless?"

She stared back at him, her eyebrow quirked up and what looked to be a challenge gleaming in her eyes. It was one of the sexiest damn things he'd seen, so it took him a minute to register what she said.

"I kissed you senseless? Well hot damn. We'll definitely be doing that again."

She laughed and as they entered the hanger, the skies opened up behind them. Taking a look around, he saw the crew packing things up for the night. Rev and Kegen were chatting off to the side. When he caught their attention, Rev lifted a hand signaling him to come over. Quin sighed and reluctantly let go. "I'll be right back."

Laurel glanced between Quin and his brothers. "I'll just get all of my stuff packed up too. I should probably be heading home anyway. It's a little bit of a drive back as you know."

Quin looked between Laurel and his brothers. He was afraid she'd take off while he was talking to them. All day long anytime she would mention leaving, he found an excuse to keep her there. It seemed like he was finally out of options. The jumps were over and he had no doubt that he had all the pictures she would need. He hesitated before making a decision he hoped would give him some more time with her as well as time to figure out how to see her again.

"Just give me a few minutes to see what they need. I still need to get that memory card out for you, then I'll walk you out when we're done."

"Oh, okay, but you know it isn't necessary to walk me out. I'm sure I can make it to my car without any help."

"It may not be necessary but I really want to."

She seemed to study him for a few seconds before her face lit up with the sweetest smile. "If you say so." She lifted on her toes and placed a gentle kiss on his lips before turning away, heading for his office.

A little bit of shock and awe hit his system. All day long he was the one that made the first move. Holding her hand. Touching her back. Pulling her next to him. Her sweet kiss on his lips was the first time she'd touched him freely. He shook off the giddy feeling that had him trapped in his spot when Kegen called his name.

He walked over knowing he was beaming like a loon. "What's up?"

Rev had a smirk on his face and Kegen grinned and shook his head.

"I think our older brother has finally been brought down, Kegen. What do you think?"

"Looks like it. I haven't seen him this taken with a woman in forever. Not even all those years with Sami, and definitely when he was with that cagey bitch Marcy."

"Whatever guys. What did you need?"

Though he was doing his best to pay attention to his brothers, he couldn't help but keep an eye on Laurel. She moved around his office gathering her gear. She looked like she belonged in there. A part of his space, his life, filled with her presence. Seeing her there did funny things to him. Her forehead scrunched up and she nibbled that delectable bottom lip again. She glanced up at him, catching his attention; the instant connection rocked him to his soul.

Rev and Kegen both started laughing, Kegen stopping before their brother. "It was nothing really. We were talking about Guys Night and grilling tomorrow. I'm pretty sure it's your turn to bring the beer." Kegen stopped and looked to where Laurel was in his office. "You can bring your girlfriend over if you want too. I'd love to see you pant after her like a lost puppy some more."

"Sure count me in, but I doubt Laurel will want to hang out with you two. What time were you thinking? We should be done with the jump around four."

"You don't know that she wouldn't be interested. You might just be afraid she will pick us over you if you let her spend more than a minute alone with us."

"Fuck you, dickhead. She would never go for your tag team style." He was also pretty confident in the groundwork he had laid today in showing he was interested in her.

"Whatever you say man. How about six-thirty?"

"Sounds good. That should give me plenty of time to head home and get cleaned up before meeting at your place."

Laurel walked out of the office then, bag slung over her shoulder and, for all intents and purposes, looking ready to leave. "Sorry to interrupt but I need to get going."

"Hey honey, you're not interrupting. We were just making plans for tomorrow."

She looked at the three of them, a ghost of a smile on her lips, and then shook her head. "That can't be good. The three of you always caused trouble when you did things together."

Quin could tell Rev and Kegen didn't remember her like he did. They had matching confused expressions on their faces and kept darting looks at him.

"They don't remember you from high school," he said.

"I would have been surprised if they did. No one really pays attention to the person behind the lens, especially in high school. It did make it easy for me to see what kind of trouble everyone got into. How do you think those photos of the Homecoming bonfire made it into the yearbook? Or the principal's reaction when he found out you guys used his stinky, old prized graduation gown to get it going?"

Quin's mouth dropped open when Laurel let out a hearty laugh. He was stunned to find out she knew about it. Kegen didn't suffer from the same stunned affliction.

"How do you know we were to blame?" Kegen may have asked the question out loud, but it was the same one going through his head.

The three of them got into a lot of trouble after their parents found out about that stunt. All of them lost their driving privileges for the rest of the school year. There was nothing quite as humiliating as having your mother drop you off and having her call out that she loves you in front of all of your friends.

"Oh Kegen, really? Everyone knew. At any rate, I did happen to be there the night you three snuck it out of his office. I had been working late on the yearbook and locking up the room."

Laurel leaned in toward Kegen, dropping her voice like she was telling a much sought after secret. "You see, I was one of those trusted students who kind of got the run of the place. I watched as you popped the lock on his office door. Rev stood watch in the hallway and Quin was the one to grab it and run. But don't worry, I never told a soul. I did make sure I was around when the principal found it missing though. Man that thing was disgusting."

Kegen threw his head back laughing. The smile on Laurel's face lit up with glee.

"Do you know who ratted us out?" Rev asked.

"Well, of course, it was Bernie Robinson. A friend of mine heard someone talking about it in the locker room. Bernie heard and went straight to the principal to turn you in. He was livid that the gown was burned. He was supposed to be the chosen student to wear it that year."

"Damn, he was a rat. I never liked that guy," Rev grumbled and they all laughed.

"Anyway, I really need to get going. I just need that memory card."

She turned toward him and held out her hand.

"Sure let me grab it out for you." Propping the helmet on his hip he popped open the camera case and fished out the little device. Handing it over he asked, "You ready to go?"

Quin wanted Laurel away from his brothers and fast. He could tell by the looks on their faces that they were seeing her in a different light. They were probably just figuring out she might be someone they wanted to pursue. What they didn't know was that he was claiming her for himself. It was going to be their loss and his gain.

He quickly slipped out of his harness and tossed it to Rev. "Thanks man." Scooping up Laurel's hand, he laced their fingers together. "Say goodbye to my brothers, Laurel."

"Huh, what?"

"Say bye." He tugged and got them moving.

"Oh! Bye Rev. Bye Kegen. Thanks for all your help."

Quin heard his brothers' laughter followed by their goodbyes as he and Laurel walked out into what was now a misty rain. Picking up speed, he had her through the gate and in her car with barely a dusting of moisture clinging to her hair.

Standing in her open door he made the split second decision to invite her to the barbecue, he just needed an opening.

"Thank you for everything, Quin. I couldn't have gotten the rest of what I needed without your help."

"You're welcome. It really was my pleasure to help out."

"Okay. Well…" She looked over to the door then back at him.

Shit. Now he was standing around looking like an idiot. *Just ask her jackass.* "I was wondering if you wanted to come to a barbecue at Rev and Kegen's place tomorrow."

She scrunched up her cute nose. "I don't know. I was going to clean my house and work on the book."

"You should take the day off. You've been busting your butt out here. I'm sure you can take a day to relax. Everything will still be there the next day."

"I know but-" She nibbled her lip and he almost lost it.

"It can be an early celebration for getting all of the pictures taken. Everything will be downhill from here, and I'm sure you have another project lined up already. I doubt you'll take the time off to recharge. Come with me, you deserve it Laurel."

She still didn't look convinced and he wasn't sure what he could do to convince her.

"A barbecue, at your brother's place? Which one?"

Dear god, she better not be interested in one of them. He had no problem setting them in an unfavorable light. "At their place. The live together. I don't think one can do anything without the other. I can't promise the place will be clean, but I can vouch that the food will be great."

"What time?"

That sounded promising. "Six-thirty. They live in that new housing development right before you get to town. The one with all of the palm trees everywhere and looks like some Florida resort."

"Oh yeah, Twin Palms. I looked at places there with a friend of mine. Seemed like a nice little community."

"So is that a yes?"

"Sure, why not. I can take a day off. It'll be nice to take a day to relax. What should I bring?"

"Just yourself. What time should I pick you up?"

"That's okay. I'll come on my own. I live on the other side of town and would hate for you to go out of your way."

Disappointment nailed him in the gut. Outwardly he smiled and leaned against the doorframe. "It wouldn't be a problem."

"Thank you for the offer, but no. I would feel more comfortable having my own car there."

"Alright then, the offer stands though if you change your mind."

"Okay. I'll need the address."

"No problem. Do you have a piece of paper and a pen?"

"Hold on." She turned from him, leaning over the console in her SUV and started rummaging through her purse, her tantalizing ass lifting off the seat, teasing him. He'd love to test how taut it was. Spank it until it turned red and she begged him to fuck her.

A frustrated noise pulled him away from the fantasy running through his head.

"Here, let me have your cell and I'll put in my number, then I can just text you the address once I get back inside."

She blew out a huff and plopped back down on her delectable derrière. "Okay."

When Laurel handed over a pink monstrosity of a phone, he couldn't help but laugh as he typed his name, number and his address in before calling his own phone so he could have hers as well.

Giving it back, he leaned inside the vehicle; he had to have one more kiss before she left, a reminder of their chemistry, not for him but for her. The kiss quickly turned heated, he had to force himself back, closing her door. It pained him to move away, but no good would come of him ravishing her in the parking lot. He would never be able to go as far as he wanted without his brothers coming to see what was taking him so long. Not to mention the rest of the crew leaving to go home.

"See you tomorrow, Laurel. Shoot me a text when you get home tonight so I know you made it okay."

She seemed flustered and a bit unsure. "Um, okay. Bye Quin and thanks again for everything."

Stepping back, he watched as she reversed then drove off. It was ridiculous how at ease he felt around her in such a short period of time and how much he missed her already.

Turning away from her retreating taillights, he headed back to the hanger, preparing to lay down the law with the two men inside. There was no way in hell he was letting them even entertain the idea that they could have Laurel.

Chapter Four

Quin gritted his teeth as Rev twirled Laurel around the patio again. Her head was tilted back and happy laughter floated through the air mixing with the soft music playing.

Ever since she arrived an hour earlier he'd barely gotten any time alone with her. It was just his bad luck she was waylaid by Kegen when she pulled into the driveway, who had been out front just finishing up mowing the lawn.

Quin swore his brother cast a quick glance to the huge bay window where he was standing and grinned. Not knowing what Kegen was up to, he stood in bewilderment as Laurel noticed when, as per his usual routine, Kegen whipped off his shirt then rinsed off with the hose. It was a habit they all formed during their youth whenever it was their turn to do the yard work. They also noticed the girls in the neighborhood stopping by to say hello to their parents on those days as well.

Before Quin could go out and rescue Laurel from Kegen's clutches, Rev called him over to help switch out the propane tank on the grill. Kegen, sans shirt, walked around the side of the house and into the backyard with Laurel's arm looped through his and her body pulled up close to his side.

Still stunned at the turn of events, he didn't even get a word out when Rev stepped up and pealed her away from his twin, claiming Kegen was getting her all hot, sweaty and wet. Laurel just laughed and let them manhandle her. The guys were either oblivious to the blush rising in her cheeks from all of the attention or were thinking of other ways they could keep that look there.

He told them in no uncertain terms over the course of the day to keep their hands and minds off her. Seems all that did was make them try harder to gain her attention.

After that, Rev and Kegen spent the next hour basically playing keep away. Quin was the sad guy in the middle and Laurel was the coveted prize. He honestly didn't know how much longer he could put up with it. And he was certain their parents wouldn't appreciate him killing their precious babies.

The song they were dancing to wound down and Laurel threw up her hands and chuckled. "Enough. I'd like to sit and relax please. I *was* promised relaxation." Her gaze flitted to where he was sitting nursing his beer.

"As you wish." Rev sketched a bow and all Quin could think about was putting a foot up his brother's ass and knocking him over.

Quin put the beer down. He was done sitting on the sidelines. "Go see if Kegen needs any help Rev. I'll take care of Laurel."

Rev smirked and Quin thought he heard him mumble, "So, the man really is interested."

He shot his brother a dirty look as he got up to snatch Laurel away. He was acting juvenile but didn't care. He beamed at Laurel, ignoring his brother standing there. "You're right, I did promise you relaxation. Did you want anything to drink?"

"A water would be fantastic. I've worked up quite the dry throat."

"Why don't you get that for her while you're checking on our brother? I'll get her settled into a nice comfy chair."

Quin was just about to gather Laurel in his arms when she spun around toward Rev. She placed a kiss on his cheek before wrapping her arms around him in a tight hug. Quin saw red and barely kept himself from exploding. "Thanks for dancing with me. I haven't done that in ages."

It was a damn good thing Laurel's back was to him. Otherwise, she would be able to see the murderous intent emanating from him. Rev only winked at him and pulled Laurel tighter against him. "Sweetheart, I'd dance with you anytime."

Quin knew that voice his brother was using. It dropped low and gravelly; he swore it revved the woman up to where they would just drop their panties at a moment's notice. Rev called it his "fuck me" voice.

Laurel didn't seem affected by it at all. Her arms tightened around Rev for a second, then she pushed back against his shoulders forcing him to let go or look like an idiot. "You are so sweet. Could I get some ice in my water please?"

All of the rage that was building up within Quin dissipated and he finally relaxed a bit. Pulling his phone from his pocket he quickly took a picture of Rev's stunned face, for future teasing or blackmailing of course. It's what brothers did when given such a great opportunity to relive a crushing blow.

Laurel turned toward him again. "Now, about that comfy chair? I wasn't expecting to be on my feet this much." She pointed down to the dainty brown sandals. Her bright red nail polish was quite the surprise and he liked it. "These were not made for so much activity. Not enough cushion."

He couldn't help but smile. Whenever she was looking at him or close to him, he felt shear happiness settle in his bones. "I have the perfect seat for you then." He would prefer she sat on his lap to keep her close and stake his claim, but didn't think she would go for it. Instead, he guided her over to the lounger next to the chair he had taken up residence in earlier. "This will let you rest those feet for a bit."

Before he let her sit, he pulled her into his arms. Any residual tension in his body all but disappeared. He rested his forehead against hers. "I don't think I've had the chance to say hello to you properly."

Unlike the hug she gave his brother, she slid her hands up his chest before twining them around his neck. It was a sensation he experienced before and it felt just as good this time, maybe even better. "I don't think so either. How are you going to fix that?"

"Like this," he whispered before placing a kiss on the tip of her nose. "And this." He dropped a kiss on one cheek, then the other. "And most definitely like this." He settled his lips on hers, pressing lightly. He wanted it to be a sweet, sensual assault. A build up of pleasure he knew they would both enjoy but was interrupted too soon by Rev…again. Brother or not, the man was really starting to get on his nerves.

"Here's your water, Laurel."

Laurel stepped back and took a seat, her toned legs stretched out in front of her, while Quin took the chair to her left. Rev handed her the drink then immediately sat on the edge of the lounger, slipping her sandals off. "I didn't mean to wear your poor little toes out." He picked up her right foot and started to rub. Her head tiled back, eyes slammed shut and a low groan escaped her lips.

Quin saw Rev's body stiffen even as he continued the massage. Quin completely understood what the sound did to his brother because it did the same to him. It made him hot and horny. Rev looked over at him, eyes wide and mouthed *holy shit*.

Laurel had unwittingly turned both of them on with a single sound. She had no clue just how sexy she was with her friendly disposition and down to earth attitude. He knew she didn't dress to be provocative yet the small brown sandals, knee length light blue flowing skirt, and brown and blue matching top exuded sensuality instead of the casual look it was meant to possess.

A shuffling noise to his left snagged his attention. Kegen stood there holding the steaks with the same look of desire Rev had etched on his face. Seemed he wasn't the only one that was seeing her in a new light.

Laurel must have sensed Kegen's presence. She lifted her head and opened her sleepy eyes. Her gaze bounced between them all. "Was I drooling or something?"

"No," Quin answered. "Why do you ask?"

"You're all staring at me strangely. I thought that maybe I fell asleep for a second, started snoring."

"I didn't realize you were that tired."

"Not tired, just finally relaxed. If you ever decide to give up skydiving Rev you would make a wonderful masseur."

"Thanks sweetheart, I'll keep that in mind in case I get tired of working with him."

Rev pointed to him and Quin snorted. "I should be so lucky."

Everyone laughed and the tension in the air evaporated.

***

Laurel stood up from the table and started gathering the dishes. It had been a wonderful evening hanging with the Ferris boys with all of the laughing and storytelling. They never talked about high school, for which she was grateful. Instead, they kept to topics that were relevant in their lives currently, such as her photography and their skydiving.

Through the course of the evening Rev flirted shamelessly with her. She was positive he did it to mess with his older brother. Kegen even got in on the fun every once in a while. For the most part, Quin would laugh and brush off what they were doing but occasionally, when he didn't think she was looking; she could see the anger and jealousy burn through his carefully created mask.

It was those times when she questioned what she thought she was doing. She accepted his invite to come over; although, never thought of it as a date, so she didn't think twice about splitting her time between the guys. Sure Quin was the one who kissed her and held her hand or found a way to keep their bodies in contact with each other. She just assumed he was attracted to her.

She glanced at her watch; at this point she wouldn't have time to find out. She needed to get going if she wanted to meet up with her friend Evan at her favorite wine bar in an hour.

"Set those down Laurel. You're still our guest," Kegen said snapping her out of her musings.

Kegen's no-nonsense tone had her setting the stack of dishes down in front of her and plopping back down in her seat, as she looked at the men around the table. "Are you sure? I don't mind helping. We go with the 'you cook, we clean' rule in my family."

"Even if you're a guest?" Kegen looked at her in question from across the table.

"Well, usually it's just with family. But…"

She never got her next words out. Rev suddenly hopped out of his chair next to her and knelt on the ground with one knee raised. "My dear, sweet Laurel does that mean you'll finally accept my marriage proposal?"

She couldn't help but laugh at his antics. All night long the stories Rev told about his two brothers made them out to be the bad guys while he was the young, innocent baby brother in all of their shenanigans. She chanced a glance at Quin, whose face seemed set in stone. She could feel a frown forming on her own face. She never expected him to be the jealous type and it was starting to tick her off.

Flashing a quick wink at Rev, she jumped up from her chair almost knocking it over. "But of course Revlin Ferris. It took all I had in me to wait this long." She clasped her hands to her chest and forced out a dreamy sigh. Nothing like the dramatics to irritate the guy you liked. Screw him if he couldn't take a joke.

Laurel screeched when Rev bolted to his feet, scooped her up in his arms and carried her to the living room, placing her on the couch where she collapsed into a fit of giggles.

He sat down next to her and leaned in. "You know my brother is dying in there?"

She tilted her head slightly and took a second to catch her breath. "Really? Which one?"

A naughty little grin kicked up the side of his mouth. If only she was attracted to him instead of the grouch in the other room. "Oh, Laurel, you are a bad one. You know exactly which brother would like to pummel me into the ground."

She studied him, the humor of the moment gone. "Why don't you explain that to me because I'm not quite sure where I stand with Quin. He invited me over but hasn't spent much time with me. He laughs right along with us yet beneath it you can see he isn't happy. He had no problem watching us dance or when I spent time with Kegen, so I wouldn't exactly call this a date."

"I can guarantee he had a problem with both of those things."

"Then why didn't he say something?"

Revlin shrugged. "I don't know."

"You want to know what I think," she whispered conspiratorially.

"Sure."

"I think he didn't say anything because he wants to like me yet, at the same time, isn't sure he should. I think he's stuck in the past where I'm the geeky *Camera Girl* and he's the popular jock."

Rev seemed to be taken aback by that, moving away a couple of inches. "Is that who you see when you look at him now? The high school jock with the ego the size of a blimp?"

"A blimp, really?"

Rev gave her a pointed look.

"No, that isn't who I see. The kid from school is long gone and I'm glad. He was hot and all, but a bit of a jerk."

He sat forward, excitement gleaming in his eyes. "Exactly! Well, not about the hot part, he's my brother and that's just weird. It's good to hear someone who agrees with me on him being a jerk. It's a very solitary stance you know."

"Have a bit of 'little brother' syndrome?"

"Nah. I like it when a woman agrees with me though."

It dawned on her then that whoever fell in love with Rev was going to have her hands full. She couldn't help but wonder if he came as a package deal with his twin. That train of thought was for a different time.

"As for your question about who I see, I just see a man who loves his family, enjoys his job, and is a guy I'd like to know better, even if I only get to be his friend."

"Uhh…you know guys can't just be friends with a woman, right? They'll think about sleeping with her at least once in their life."

"You're such a dork, Rev."

He laughed and slumped against the back of the couch pulling her with him. "You really are a special woman Laurel. Makes me wonder if I had a chance with you in high school and why I never noticed you back then."

She patted him in a brotherly fashion on the chest. "Sorry Rev. Back then I was invisible. At least that's how I felt. As for my affections, well they have always belonged to Quin. Then and I'm afraid to say…now."

Quin took that exact moment to walk into the room. What he saw didn't take the scowl off his face; it only made it deeper. His lips thinned, jaw clenched and nostrils flared in irritation. If the situation had been reversed, she probably wouldn't have liked it either.

Instead of saying anything to them, though, he walked out the front door, slamming it closed behind him. She could see him through the bay window pacing back and forth before he disappeared down the driveway.

Kegen raced into the room and saw what Quin had just walked in on. "Fuck."

Laurel bolted upright. "Oh dear."

Rev kissed her on the cheek. "Stay here sweetheart. I'll go calm him down. I think we might have pushed him too much tonight, me especially. We both knew he was into you. Hell, he even told us to stay away from you."

She got up from the couch and searched for her purse, finding it on the table next to the front door. "I should probably head out anyway. I'm supposed to meet a friend tonight. He made an unexpected trip to town today and wanted to meet up."

That pulled Rev and Kegen up short. Rev spoke first. "You have a date with another man? Why would you make another date when you knew you were going out with Quin? Maybe you aren't the one for our brother after all."

Laurel looked between the twins, completely confused by the one-eighty. "You sound like a woman, you know that right?" When they both just glared at her she shook her head in frustration. "I knew there was a reason I didn't date. Just can't figure guys out at all." She grabbed her purse, heading the same direction Quin just went.

Kegen grabbed her by the arm and spun her around before she reached the doorknob. "Okay, explain that."

"I don't have to explain anything, but since I thought we were on our way to being friends, I will. First, I don't think this little get-together can be considered a date. The man barely talked to me tonight. Kissed yes, shot you two dirty looks, yes, talked to me, no. Second, I don't have a *date* with another man. I'm meeting a friend I've known since college, who happens to be a man, at the wine bar in town. I have no desire to date, sleep with or fuck Evan. We are just old college friends and colleagues."

Rev looked unconvinced. "Sweetheart, remember when I said all men think of sleeping with a woman at least once?"

She couldn't help but roll her eyes at his idiotic words. "Yes, but just because he may have thought about it, doesn't mean I'm going to do it. Or does that not factor into your man-equation?"

Rumbling from a large truck startled her into action. "I'm outta here. Thank you for the help at the jumps. Thank you for dinner. I hope you have a nice life."

Before Rev or Kegen could stop her, she yanked the front door open. Quin was just sitting in his truck staring at the house. Beyond irritated at all three men, she jogged to her SUV, hopped in and backed-up, barely avoiding ramming into Quin's truck. Throwing the vehicle into gear she stomped on the gas pedal, peeling out of the quite neighborhood. If she ever heard from those guys again it would be too soon.

Chapter Five

Quin's heart stopped in his chest as Laurel came within inches of hitting his truck. He didn't know if it was because she almost hit him, or if it was seeing her leaving without being able to talk to her. He knew he fucked up storming out of the house. He'd been so pissed at his brother, then got even more pissed when he saw her snuggled up to him. It was either bust his brother in the face or leave. He would have been screwed no matter what he decided.

The squeal of tires grabbed his attention and he could only watch as Laurel tore out like a bat out of Hell. He cut the engine of his truck and got out, making his way over to where his brothers stood on the front porch.

"What the fuck did you do to her?" He demanded, grabbing Rev by the shirt. Rev immediately pushed back at him but Quin didn't let go.

"I didn't do shit to her asshole. You're the one who left the house like a two-year-old who's had his favorite toy taken away."

"Fuck you!" He shoved Rev back, causing him to stumble. "I saw you two snuggled up on the couch then, next thing I know, she's tearing out of here like she can't get away fast enough."

"If you call that snuggled up then you haven't been doing it right. We were sitting next to each other, talking. Which is more than I can say you did. She even commented about it. What the hell did you invite her over for if you weren't going to make a move or at least talk to her?"

"How was I supposed to when all night long you and Kegen were flirting with her, hogging all of her attention? You knew I wanted her. I even told you to back off. Instead of respecting my request, you spent the evening trying to take her from me."

"Holy shit! Are you serious? You demanded we stay away from her. Did you honestly think we wouldn't take that as a challenge? We've been screwing with you all night, just having a bit of fun. Laurel never took any of it seriously. It isn't my fault you can't handle a harmless bit of fun."

Kegen stepped between them. "Enough! Both of you need to get your asses inside. The last thing we need is for the neighbors to call the cops because you two are having a yelling match in the front yard. Mom and Dad would skin us *all* alive if that happened."

Rev spun away without another word, followed by Kegen.

Quin stood out front lost on his thoughts staring at the spot where Laurel used to be parked. He didn't think he needed to tell Rev and Kegen how important this night was. The fact that he asked her to come to their usual Saturday Guys Night get-together should have been enough. In truth, he didn't quite understand how important it was either until it went horribly wrong.

He must have been outside longer than he thought. Rev poked his head out the front door. "You coming in or what? Mom dropped off her famous coconut crème pie earlier. We're ready to eat it."

Studying his youngest brother, a wave of guilt enveloped him. He knew better than to take his frustrations out on Rev. He should have been able to handle the teasing and flirting. He would have done the same thing if one of his brothers had told him to keep away from a beautiful woman.

"Hey Rev?" He waited until he had his full attention. "Sorry about earlier. I'm tied up in knots about that woman. There's just something about her that makes me want more."

"Yeah. I get it. She's special and I hate to say this because it will give you a big ego, but she's not for Kegen or me. She's only got eyes for your stupid ass. At least that's what she told me right before you lost your shit."

Surprise at hearing those words grabbed him by the balls. "Seriously? You're not fucking with me now are you?"

"Nah. I asked if I'd ever have a chance with her. She told me no. For some idiotic reason all of her affections, past and present, belong to you. Though, I have to tell you, she's just not sure where she stands with you. You've got her pretty confused so I'm thinking you need to work on that. I'd hate to see you ruin something that could be the best thing you'll ever come across."

Rev disappeared into the house again. Before he could join his brothers he needed to do one thing. Pulling his phone from his pocket he texted Laurel.

Quin: *Sorry I was an ass. Call me. Want to make it up to you.*

Shoving the phone back in his pocket he went inside and tried to patiently wait for a reply. It became apparent after a couple of minutes he wasn't very good at that.

Kegen stood in front of him shaking his head in disgust while holding out a plate of pie. "Bro, stop looking at your phone. She just left and she's driving. I doubt she's going to text you back right this minute. She seems like the responsible sort. Probably stops at railroad crossing even if there's no sign of a train."

Rev with a mouthful of food mumbled, "She was pretty ticked when she left. I have a feeling she thinks all men are idiots."

Quin looked over at his brother. "What happened to piss her off anyway? It can't just be my fault."

"Nope. I blame most of it on dipshit over there." Kegen pointed to Rev as he took a seat in the recliner, "He got all butt hurt when she said she was meeting someone at the wine bar."

"Why would that make you upset? So she was meeting a friend. Hell, maybe it's someone you two could date." Unless there was more to the story Rev wasn't telling him. The bite of pie he just swallowed curdled in his stomach. He had a sinking feeling he wasn't going to like what came next.

Rev cleared his throat. "A guy friend. One she has known since college and I'm guessing likes enough to maintain a friendship with."

"She made a date with another guy? Fuck that!" Quin bolted up off the couch, mindlessly looking for his truck keys.

"Dude, chill."

Quin couldn't believe how laid-back Kegen was being. Of course, this wasn't a woman *he* was trying to date.

"Is she not going to meet with another guy at a predetermined spot at a predetermined time? Is that not the definition of a date?"

Kegen looked up at him with amusement in his eyes. His lips twitched in the makings of a smile. "Now that you put it that way, then yep, she's on a date."

Snorting sounds behind him had him spinning around. Revlin was doubled over in laughter. "What in the fuck are you laughing about?"

"Kegen's right. She's on a date and there isn't a thing you can do about it."

"The hell I can't."

"The hell you won't. You show up at the bar and she's likely to throw something at your head. She's already pissed at all of us. I don't think you want to give her more ammunition to be mad. You need to give her a minute to cool down. I'm thinking texting her isn't going to help either." Rev got up from his seat and ambled into the kitchen. Quin would never admit it out loud, but Rev was right. If he pushed her too hard, he really believed she would slam the door in his face.

"Fuck me. I can't sit around here and wait for her to get back to me." He flopped back on the couch.

"What other choice do you have?" Kegen asked.

"I'll think of something." And he better do it quick.

***

Laurel pulled up at the wine bar with thirty minutes to spare. She pulled her phone out to text Evan and let him know she was early, only to get distracted by a message from Quin.

Quin: *Sorry I was an ass. Call me. Want to make it up to you.*

"Make it up to me. Ha! I don't know if you're worth the trouble Quinton Ferris." Her irritation at him burned just as much as it did for his brothers, actually more. They knew what they were doing when they taunted him. Quin, on the other hand, if he was so interested should have stepped up to the plate and put a stop to their games.

"MEN!"

A loud rap on her window jerked her out of her musings, scaring her. Standing on the other side of the window was Evan, his trademark smile lighting up his face.

Cutting the engine she grabbed her purse and phone, glancing down at Quin's text glaring back at her. She nibbled her lip, unable to decide if she should text him back and tell him to get lost or just wait and see how she felt in the morning.

"Laurel? Something wrong?"

She shook her head and got out. Quin was just going to have to wait until morning. That is if she was in a better mood. "No, nothing wrong. I was just about to text you and let you know I was here early."

Evan pulled her into hug, wrapping his beefy arms around her. You would never know by looking at him that he was the photographer and not the model.

He pulled back and seemed to search her face. She had no idea what he was looking for. Maybe he was trying to gauge her mood, which at the moment was pretty shitty but starting to look up.

He dropped a kiss on her head then tucked her beneath his arm. "I must be psychic then or just hungry. I've missed the hell out of you."

She laughed and clung to Evan, as his long legs ate up the sidewalk. The only way for her to keep up with this stride was to hold on and let him practically carry her. Thank goodness he was strong enough to bear her weight.

Twenty minutes later they were seated in one of the intimate corner booths. Every time she moved, she bumped into Evan's leg or arm. He only laughed the more frustrated she got.

"Seriously, these tables are too damn small. How are you supposed to get more than one plate on here?"

Laurel pushed the cheese platter to the side knocking it into the bottle of wine as the waiter put down Evan's plate. Evan barely caught the bottle before it tipped. He waited for the server to leave.

"Well, I'm thinking they expect you to be romantic and share plates back here."

She knew she was pouting and getting grumpier by the minute. When they first walked into the wine bar the previous few hours had drifted away and the comfort she always felt with Evan settled in. Then he started looking at her in a different way, like he was studying her, checking her reactions to things he would say or do. He would also, what she suspected was supposed to be casual, brush his fingers over her hand or lean in while resting his hand on her back. He kept touching her the same way Quin had yesterday yet instead of the giddy, feminine feeling, it just felt wrong.

"We could have waited for another table to clear up," she grumbled.

"I'm pretty certain I would have died of starvation by then. Look at me, I'm skin and bones."

Laurel couldn't help the guffaw she made. "Evan you have never been skin and bones. You might be the fittest man I know."

The flash of a memory of Quin standing in front of her with his shirt off made her pause. *Well, maybe not the fittest.*

"You say the sweetest things, peaches. We'll be fine at this table. There's plenty of room. Here." He lifted his left arm and motioned for her to move closer. Reluctantly she inched next to him and jolted when he draped his arm across her shoulders.

"What's got you all worked up tonight? You're usually the most patient, accommodating woman I know."

"I am not worked up. Just a little grumpy. I had a long day on very little sleep."

"Come on Laurel, this is me you're talking to. How long have we been friends?"

Picking up her glass of wine, she drained the last bits while figuring it out. "Damn, have we really known each other for eight years?"

Evan laughed and she found it soothing. "Yep. Eight long years."

"Whatever." She punched him in the stomach lightly and relaxed a bit into him. "You know you're thankful to have me as a friend."

Evan scooped up a bite of pasta and held it out for her. Without thought she opened her mouth and let him feed her.

He snorted as he took a bite of pasta for himself.

"I've always been glad we're friends, so why don't you tell me what's up?"

Laurel held out her glass and waited for him to refill it. She didn't have to debate long about telling Evan about Quin. It would actually be nice to talk to someone not invested in the outcome.

"There's this guy."

"Damn, I never would have guessed that." Evan sounded surprised to hear it. She was kind of offended by his reaction.

"I date," she said a bit too defensively, even to her own ears.

Evan looked at her skeptically. "Yeah, not so much hun."

She couldn't stop the roll of her eyes. "Anyway, there's this guy and I used to know him back in high school. Well, I didn't really know him. He was popular, I wasn't. I had a HUGE crush on him and nothing ever came of it. After graduation I went my way, he went his way." She stopped and took a gulp of wine, deciding to skip over the embarrassing events that shaped her life.

"I have a feeling there's more to it but go on."

"I have that skydiving look-book assignment."

"Yeah. We emailed back and forth about it. I think you should be doing other things, but you enjoy niche projects."

She patted him on the knee, belatedly feeling his leg stiffen when she moved her hand away. "Yes, I know. Back to my story. I went out to the Chute Shack with Jason and his friends and found out that this guy, the one from high school, owns the place with his brothers. I don't think he knew who I was at first. He seemed attracted to me and I'm attracted to him, even after all of these years. So he invites me to his brothers' place, but I don't see it as a real date. We had a good time laughing and talking, then he freaked out when one of his brothers carried me off into the other room as a joke. The brothers ended up pissing *me* off by saying I'm two-timing Quin with you."

"Whoa, when did all of this happen and how am I involved?"

"Tonight. I came straight from their place to here. It's why I was early. I was mad and left. You're involved because I said I was getting together with a friend and colleague, who happened to be a guy."

"I see. So they think you made a date with two men for the same night."

"But see, that's the thing. I don't see either one as a date."

Evan pulled his arm off her shoulders and shifted away. The warmth he exuded earlier shifted to cold indifference.

"Let me ask you something, Laurel."

"Okay."

"Why don't you see this," he motioned between them, "as being a date?"

"Uh, because we're friends and don't think of each other in a romantic way. At least I don't, and I assumed if you did, you would have said something by now."

"Okay, I'll get back to that. We need to back up a minute. When did you agree to go out with Quin?"

"Last Sunday."

"When did you agree to meet me?"

"This morning."

"So even though you knew you would be going out with this guy and you didn't know how long you would be there or what would happen, you made a *date* to meet me here?"

"Well, when you put it like that." Now all she felt was guilty. She didn't think about the fact that she and Quin could have really hit it off and might want to spend the evening together. She just thought in her naïve brain that he was just being friendly. Completely discounting the kissing and touching, and the way he still made her heart trip.

"Yeah. Now, back to thinking of you in a romantic way. Maybe I have all along."

The blood drained from her face. "What! But you've never given me any indication that you did." Rev's words from earlier picked that moment to haunt her. *Guys can't just be friends with a woman. They think about sleeping with them at least once.*

Evan had the audacity to laugh.

"I said maybe, Laurel. I've always felt there was something holding you back from seeing me as more. From listening to you talk and watching your eyes light up, that something is this guy Quin."

Laurel scrambled out of the seat. "Oh my god!" She clamped her hand over her mouth. Shocked at his declaration as much as him pointing out her hang up on Quin.

"You don't need to look so horrified." His lips tipped up slightly on one side in a half smile.

"I'm sorry, I just never would have guessed." *To any of it.* She thought she'd gotten over Quin years ago.

Evan reached over and grabbed her hand, pulling her back onto the seat. "It's really okay, Laurel. I only said maybe. I might have felt that way at one time when we first met but I don't anymore."

She wasn't so sure she believed him. Something passed behind his eyes when she said she never thought of him being more than a friend.

"Peaches, I've always been attracted to you but I value our friendship more."

She tried to pull away again. She was still reeling and she didn't want to hurt him any more by staying.

"You're not running off. It's good we finally talked about it, and I am happy there is someone who makes your eyes sparkle."

"I'm not so sure this was a good thing. I...I really never thought of you as boyfriend material. I don't want to hurt you but it's the truth. I love having you as a friend and I'm afraid this will change everything."

Evan shrugged then picked up his fork. "It might change it a little but," he paused, taking a bite and swallowing before continuing on, "I'm actually fine. My heart isn't really broken, my ego a bit bruised, but my heart is okay."

Laurel didn't know if she could say the same thing.

Chapter Six

Laurel and Evan, actually mostly Laurel, polished off the second bottle of wine. After his revelation about his old feelings for her and her feelings for Quin, she couldn't down the stuff quick enough. Eventually, she was able to get back to the comfortable companionship they had before.

Evan truly wasn't that upset about the evening's events. He even admitted he was fond of her, although never thought himself in love with her.

When it was time to go, it was decided that she would leave her SUV at the wine bar and Evan would take her home. She'd had plenty to drink and was in no condition to get behind the wheel.

"Thanks again for the ride, Evan. I could have walked," she slurred while sitting in the passenger seat of his sports car. He had the top down and the cool night air felt fantastic on her flushed face.

"Friends don't let friends drink and walk home alone."

"Hmm, that's nice."

"I'm sorry I let you have too much. I should have paid more attention once you settled down. I'm afraid I would have made a terrible boyfriend."

"Oh Evan, you're a handsome man," she sighed, "but just not for me." She tipped over landing face first in his lap as he rounded the corner onto her street.

"Oops," she hiccuped. As she attempted to push herself up, her hand slipped off his thigh, her face landing hard onto his groin. His grunt had her giggling as he stopped the car.

She felt a shadow fall over her.

"What in the hell is going on?" A voice that sounded just like Quin's came out of nowhere.

"He can't be here. He doesn't know where I live." The words were lost in the crotch her face currently resided.

She tried one more time to get up and when her hand slipped again, she expected to get another face full of denim, and just when she would have made impact she was dragged back.

The person holding her up turned her towards them. She squinted her eyes to make them focus, but it was no use. The person in front of her was a blurry mass of man. He opened the door and squatted down in front of her.

"You must be Quin," Evan boomed over her head.

"Hey, not so loud, my head kinda hurts." She batted a hand in his direction and came up empty.

"Yeah, I'm Quin. Who the hell are you and why is she so damn drunk?"

"Name's Evan Freemont. I'm an old friend of Laurel's from college. She's drunk because she had too much wine and not enough food tonight. Seems she had kind of a crap evening before we hooked up and things didn't get much better."

"You're the guy she had a date with after the one with me." Quin's deep voice sounded so angry. She didn't like that. She also didn't like Evan saying they hooked up.

She turned her head in what she thought was his direction, she wobbled in her seat before the hands on her shoulders steadied her. "We did not hook up Evan. Remember, I told you there was someone else. Hell if I can tell what he wants but I want to be with him, not you."

Evan chuckled lightly. "Oh, peaches, you say the sweetest things to me." A featherweight kiss landed on the top of her head.

"Listen Quin, I don't know you but I do know Laurel. She's got a soft and loving heart and if you break it in any way, I'll come after your ass and make you feel the same pain."

"You don't need to threaten me. I wouldn't do anything to hurt her." Evan had all but growled the words.

"Again."

"What?" both men shouted.

"I guess I didn't say that in my head then. I'm so very sleepy."

"I've got ya honey."

She was lifted out of the seat. Strong arms supported her back and under her knees as she leaned into a hot, muscular chest. She took a deep breath and inhaled the subtle outdoor scent that could only belong to Quin.

"I guess I have no choice since she picked you. A word of advice though, let her know how you feel and do whatever you have to in order to make her happy. If you don't, I won't have a problem coming back to convince her to give me a shot."

Closing her eyes she fell asleep on the short walk to her door, only to be awakened by two men whispering. A door closed and soon she was being relieved of all of her restrictive clothing and placed under her cool sheets.

The bed dipped next to her and she had a moment's panic. Her arm flew out but was caught before she made contact.

"It's just me honey." Her arm was folded across her belly. "You're fine. Just get some rest. I'll be here when you wake up."

She wanted to tell him she was glad he was there, but sleep pulled her under before she could form the words.

***

Quin picked up his cell on the third ring as he stepped out of the hanger, not bothering to look at the caller ID. The only calls he got on his cell during the day were from his Mom, who was on vacation in Alaska with their Dad, and now Laurel.

After she woke up Sunday morning with a killer headache, Quin started a hot shower for her, watching over her as she got in. It killed him to see all of that naked flesh and be unable to do anything about it, but he made a vow to himself that night.

He decided, while he impatiently waited in her driveway for her to get home, to take it slow and steady with her. She was the type of woman who deserved romance and wining and dining. However, after the state she came home in, he was now going to leave the wining out.

When she dragged herself out of the shower a half hour later, snuggled up in sweats and a tank top, his urge to ravish her hadn't diminished. Instead of acting on his raging hormones, he made sure she took two aspirin and forced her to eat some toast and drink a little coffee.

He coaxed her into making a quick call to her parents to let them know she was okay, then he tucked her back in bed, making sure she had a gallon of water by her side.

He left her there with a kiss on the forehead and a promise to check on her later, which he did via text and phone. He couldn't trust himself to spend another day and night with her curled around him and not want to make love to her. She was going to get the full treatment from him so there would be no mistaking what he wanted from her.

They called and texted a couple times each day now. Sometimes right before bed. Others when they were done with work. Each time they talked, they tried to find time to see each other but their schedules weren't allowing for it.

"Hello."

"Hey Quin."

Laurel's happy voice rushed over the line, the sound filling him with bliss. He glanced down at his watch to check the time, surprised to find it was only noon. "Hey honey, how's work? I didn't expect to hear from you this early."

"I grabbed a few minutes for lunch and, I don't know, just thought I'd call. See how your day was going. I figured I would be talking to your voicemail."

"We just finished with a group of tandem jumps. They were the only ones scheduled, so I'm going to head in and get some paperwork done while the crew cleans things up around here."

There was rustling and hushed voices on Laurel's end. "That's great."

"You sound distracted. What's going on there?"

"A bride can't find her veil. They're searching everywhere, including under me. Like I wouldn't notice sitting on a six-foot piece of lace."

"I'm going to guess that it would be kind of hard to miss."

"Yeah. So I was wondering." Her words trailed off. "Never mind.

"No, not never mind. What were you wondering?"

"It's okay, I forgot you said yesterday that you were getting together tomorrow with your brothers like you always do."

He switched the phone to his other ear and leaned against the wall. It was quieter outside, easier to pretend he was alone with Laurel and not ten feet away from a gaggle of overly excited jumpers. "We're only getting together for some grub, just like last week. Nothing big. Now tell me, what were you thinking?"

"I was just wondering if you wanted to come to my place tomorrow and preview the book. I could really use your vast amount of knowledge with some of the descriptions to finish it up. I was thinking if we scheduled it like work, we would be able to finally see each other again."

Quin didn't need any time to think about it. He knew the second she uttered the words *come to my place* that he was going to make it work. With any luck, he'd finally be able to put his plan in motion of letting her know he was very serious about them being a couple. No matter how often he talked to her on the phone, he had the feeling that she wasn't quite convinced yet.

"Trust me, I have no problem bailing on Rev and Kegen. I know they'll understand. What time were you thinking?"

She laughed and the sound went straight to his head. The soft sound coming from her was so light and filled with joy. He had never heard anything like it. "How about ten? I've got to meet Evan for breakfast so I can say goodbye."

Quin waited for the quick stab of jealousy at hearing Evan's name to die down. They talked about Evan and she explained their relationship. Still, Quin didn't trust the guy and who would blame him. He all but said if Quin didn't make her happy, then he was coming back for her. "Ten should be fine. Wait, no. We have a client in the morning. We probably won't be done with them until around four. We planned to get together at six-thirty again."

"Oh, okay then. It was worth a shot. I'll just complete it on my own and maybe we can find another time to go on a date."

Panic raced across his heart. He didn't want to let this opportunity to see her pass. "Hold on, how about Sunday?"

"No. Can't do it. Remember, I have a brunch date with my parents, then shopping with my Mom since I flaked out on them last weekend. Besides, you really don't want to subject yourself to their interrogation. Which I can assure you they will do and you will run screaming at the first opportunity."

"Really? At the first opportunity? How many guys have your parents run off? Wait, no. Don't answer that. I don't want to know."

"I can assure you there haven't been that many. None of them ever called back though. I'd like a little more time with you before the inevitable happens."

"Have a little faith in me honey. Those other guys just weren't the right ones for you. You'll see I'm made of much stronger stuff."

"Promises, promises," she laughed

Her laughter only made him want to prove he was right.

"So, back to getting a date with you even if you are trying to disguise it as work. How about I skip the barbecue and come over instead? After six isn't too late is it?"

He could practically hear her thinking on the other end of the line "Sure that sounds like a good idea. Since you'll be missing dinner with your brothers, how about I cook something up for us?"

He felt a smile take over his face. "I'd like that. I'll see you around six-thirty then?"

"Sounds like a date." There was a muffled noise on Laurel's end. "Gotta go. Work is calling my name. I'll talk to you later Quin. Bye."

Laurel hung up before he could say goodbye. She seemed to do that a lot. Once it was time to work, she was gone. Pulling up his messages, he sent her a quick text.

Don't work too hard. Can't wait to see you Saturday night. ~ Quin

He walked back into the hanger and called his brothers in. No time like the present to let them know, Guys Night was officially over.

Chapter Seven

Laurel rushed around the house making sure everything was in its place and cleaned within an inch of its life. The place needed to be perfect. Granted, he had been in the house before, but she liked to pretend that embarrassing incident never happened. Getting drunk, not knowing for sure how you got home, and then waking up to your dream guy and wondering if you were going to puke was not good.

Laurel fluffed a decorative chair pillow for the third time as she glanced at the huge clock hanging over her mantel, seven o'clock.

"He isn't going to show up."

No, that can't be right. They had finally arranged their schedules. Okay, so it sucked that they had to pencil time in but, if things worked out, they would find a way to be together more.

Just then the doorbell rang, causing Laurel to jump in surprise and bang into the coffee table. "Shit!"

Rubbing the spot on her shin she rushed to the door, taking a second to stop in front of the mirror on the wall and smooth her hair. With a deep breath to calm her nerves, she turned the deadbolt and opened the door.

That deep breath she had just taken – well, it came out in a giant rush. Quin stood in front of her, sexy grin curving one side of his lips and amusement twinkling in his dark brown eyes. His black hair ruffled in the breeze, a wayward lock brushing his forehead.

Laurel's gaze traveled lower. He wore a dark blue t-shirt that clung to his broad shoulders and hung loose at his waist right above a pair of black cargo shorts.

"Is there a problem? I thought I heard you curse."

"Huh, what?" She glanced up to look into his eyes. A blush quickly warming her cheeks at being caught staring. She shouldn't feel this shy around him. "Oh no. It was nothing. Just surprised when I heard the bell ring. I was beginning to think you weren't coming and I got to straightening things again then smashed into the coffee table."

Great...now she was babbling.

Quin's warm chuckle danced across her senses. It was deep and rich, sending shivers down her spine. Completely lost in the sound, her habit of nibbling on her bottom lip kicked in. Damn the man was even more enticing than the teenage boy she had known.

A low groan rumbling from his chest grabbed her attention. Before she could process what it was about, Quin hooked her around the waist and pulled her in tight, slamming his lips down on hers in a heated kiss. He swiped his tongue along the seam, dragging a moan from within her. Her mouth opened giving him access, delighted when his grip tightened and she felt his cock harden against her.

Abruptly he pulled away but didn't release her. "It might be a good idea to invite me in. The things I want to do to you shouldn't be done in front of your neighbors. Unless, of course, you don't mind a bit of PDS."

"PDS? I've heard of PDA, public display of affection."

"Publicly displayed sex."

"Oh! Um. Why don't you come in then?"

With his arms wrapped tightly around her, he walked her backwards through the door, slamming it behind him. Leaning back he fused their bodies together, crushing her aching breasts against his chest. Zings of pleasure erupted through her body as he seduced her with his mouth again. One of his large hands skimmed down her waist, grabbing her ass he pulled her harder against him. His free hand plowed through her hair before cupping the back of her head, holding her in place as he assaulted her mouth, sending her hormones into overdrive. The insistent throbbing of her clit told her she needed more.

She didn't know if she should demand he take her to bed and fuck her or get on with the reason she invited him over; to work on finishing up her latest assignment. Laurel was sure he wouldn't have a problem with the first, but she really needed to focus on work. Coming up for air, she pushed slightly against his shoulders. "We need to stop," she panted.

"Not sure I can." He set his lips against her neck and nibbled. "I've been wanting to get my hands back on you since I left last Sunday. I'm finding you rather irresistible."

Her brain turned to mush, thoughts about work almost escaping her. "Mmm…. I like that but we have work to do. I need to get this assignment done and I have a feeling if we don't stop now, we'll never get back to the reason you came over."

"I came over for more than just helping you out Laurel." He nipped her bottom lip eliciting a sharp sting that turned her on.

"Oh!"

Her shock must have sunk in. He looked at her questioningly. "You do know I'm interested in more, right? And not just sex."

A couple of minutes passed by in awkward silence before Laurel nodded her head. She did know that in her gut but was too afraid to think it. What if she'd been wrong? What if the flirty phone calls and texts weren't that? What if he was stringing her along until the book was done and he made sure they were properly credited?

"Do you want something to drink?" Spinning around she broke Quin's hold, making a mad dash for the kitchen while leaving him to decide if he wanted to follow.

Damn, she didn't know what she wanted to do now. The need to finish the look-book battled with arousal and her need to sate it. A plan formed in her head. She needed to make this about business and forget the heart throbbing, overwhelming elation she felt when he was around. When they were done, she could freely seduce him into her bed without thinking this was about something else and see how long she could keep him there.

Yanking the fridge door open, she poked her head inside in a lame attempt to cool down as he walked into the kitchen. "I've got sweet tea, soda or water. If you're in the mood for coffee, I have plenty of that but it'll take a couple minutes to brew."

"Sweet tea will be fine."

She pulled the jug out, setting it on the counter. Grabbing up two glass tumblers, she filled them with ice before pouring the tea. Every little step helping her calm down and firming her resolve to work first, play later. She handed a tumbler to Quin and took a quick sip of her own. She bit her lip to keep from groaning out loud as he drained the glass, tipping his head back. She wanted to lick her way up his neck before tasting the sweet tea on his lips.

Keep your mind on business. The fun stuff can come later. She cleared her throat. "So, I pretty much have the book all put together. Why don't we head to my office so you can see?"

Slipping by him, she silently made her way down the hall and into the one room she spent the majority of her time. She really should put a better bed in here though. The futon just wasn't cutting it on those days when she was too tired to walk the extra few feet to her bedroom.

Two steps in the door and a wave of nausea hit her. The silver framed photograph she pulled out earlier in the day taunted her as it sat in plain view. She couldn't believe she forgot it was out.

She glared at it, hoping it would vanish before Quin caught sight. It was the last picture she ever took of him while in school. As painful as the moment had been for her, when she first saw the image she knew she would get it printed. It was the one and only picture she physically had in her possession, regardless of what the rumors had been.

While going through the images from the jump, she found she had fallen into the old pattern of taking pictures of him while he wasn't looking. Stumbling across one that reminded her of the one from school, she wanted to compare the two images: The one on the computer screen and the one in the frame. She had been completely caught in the moment.

If only she had put them away and not left them both in plain sight.

Laurel sensed Quin walking in behind her just as she realized her mistake. How guilty would she look if she rushed in and scooped up the frame and tossed it in the bottom drawer of the desk? Probably pretty guilty or at least obvious that something was going on. If she could just make it a couple more steps before he noticed then she'd be golden. She could casually lay the frame down like it was no big deal. Her eyes skittered to the sleeping monitor, not much she could do about that. She just needed to make sure they didn't bump it and wake the damn thing up.

She took another step forward when he slipped his arms around her waist and nuzzled her neck, stopping her in her tracks.

"You seem a little up-tight, almost nervous Laurel." He placed a trail of kisses down the side of her neck.

"I am." Now she couldn't move at all. His lips on her neck were inciting a riot of tingles across her skin. Her nipples beaded, pressing against the satin of her bra, seeming to reach out for attention, while a small shiver worked its way down her spine.

"No reason to be nervous with me honey. I'm the same guy I was out at the Shack; the same guy who tucked you in and watched over you during the night. We won't do anything you don't want to. We can just work on the book if that's what you want. Spend time getting to know one another."

Laurel's laugh came out strangled. Not do anything? The man was crazy. Her body was turning against her brain and ramping up with need. It wanted more from him while her brain demanded the picture needed to be taken care of. "I know you're the same guy. It's just that this feels different."

He spun her around, walking her backward a couple steps and bumping the desk behind her knocking the frame down. Neither paid much attention to it. "No it isn't. We are the same people as before. I happen to think there's a mutual attraction going on and I'd like to explore it. The only thing that's different is that we're finally all alone."

Swooping in he placed soft, gentle kisses on her lips. She didn't know if he was trying to coax her to relax or trying to lure her into submission with quiet understanding. Either way, he was getting her mind off her dilemma.

She melted into his hard body, pressing her aching breasts against his chest. Slipping her fingers up his arms, she felt the flexing and bunching of hard, sinewy muscles along the way. Finally reaching his head, she tunneled her fingers into his hair. Gripping it in her fists as she increased the pressure of her lips against his. He pulled her closer as though trying to meld their bodies together.

For long minutes they delved into each other's mouths exploring every aspect while their tongues slid against each other. Quin was the first to pull away, panting heavily.

She knew the minute he spotted the picture. His body stiffened and he took a step back before moving her to the side.

The monitor glowed brightly at them, having come alive when they bumped the desk. The frame with his picture, instead of falling face down, had fallen back leaving his handsome visage staring up at them.

She glanced at Quin, who stood unmoving, jaw clenched, then to the computer and the frame. She could admit this didn't look good for her. She looked like the lovesick fool everyone claimed she was years ago. Still, she couldn't help but think that no matter what expression was on display, he was a good-looking man. Too bad she screwed it up already.

Laurel placed her hand on Quin's arm. "I can explain," she said softly.

Quin peered at her, a questioning expression on his face.

***

Quin's eyes were drawn back to the frame holding a picture of him from high school. He recognized immediately when it was taken. A day he tried his hardest to forget and for a while had. It wasn't until Laurel started coming out to the Shack that it pricked at his conscience. He didn't even connect the two events together until his brother mentioned *Camera Girl*, then it hit him like a freight train.

For the life of him he didn't know why she had the picture. It had to be a bad memory for her.

"Why?" He blurted the question out without thought.

Laurel fidgeted next to him, her head was dipped low, hands clenched so tightly her knuckles were turning white. "It was a habit. I didn't even think twice about snapping your picture when you weren't looking. When I was going through everything on the memory card, it reminded me of the one in the frame. I got the old one out to see them together. Just so you know, I'm not some kind of stalker or lovesick fool. It was purely coincidence."

He turned toward her more confused than ever. "What? I meant why do you even have that picture in the frame?"

A bright red blush crept up Laurel's cheeks. "This is really embarrassing. I'm not sure I want to go there."

"You're stalling Laurel. Why would you have something that can't possibly hold any good memories?"

Her head popped up so quickly he was surprised she didn't get whiplash. "You remember?"

"Yes."

"You remember the day that was taken?" She sounded skeptical and he wasn't sure he liked that. He wasn't an idiot, well, at least not these days; teenage him was a bit of one at the time.

"I told you I do. Now answer my question. Why do you have that photo?" He knew he should feel bad that he was pushing her. It was obvious this was something she wanted to avoid. He could see that she expected him to be mad. To be honest he wasn't, shocked sure, but not mad. There was something driving him to hear the story, something that was telling him this was important for both of them.

She seemed to study him for a moment, nibbling on that damn delectable bottom lip. He repressed the groan trying to escape while he waited for his answer. She didn't need to know he was turned on at the moment. He was oddly flattered she still had the old picture and that she fell into the habit of taking his picture. It meant she was still attracted to him and he'd take that, build on it to make something more.

She pointed to the futon behind him. "Please have a seat." While he didn't want to, if it meant he was going to get his answer without further argument or stall tactics, he would do it.

Laurel walked to the desk and picked up the frame, dropping her gaze to the picture. "You have to promise you'll hear me out without interrupting. It's probably the only way I'll get it all out there. You do have the right to know why your face seems to be plastered all over the computer and why I have a framed print of you."

"It can't be that bad."

"Really? Everyone either called me *Lovesick Laurel* or *Camera Girl* after that day." She wrinkled her nose before she shook the frame in her hands. "This kind of proves they were right about both."

He studied her for a moment. Her shoulders looked tense, brow was furrowed. It really did bother her to relive it all. She still carried the humiliation that followed that fateful day; though, looking at her now you wouldn't know it. At the thought, a sudden flash of guilt swept through him. It was because of him she had to endure those nicknames. "I'd really like to know, Laurel."

She gave a quick nod of her head. "This was the very last picture I ever took of you, until recently. It was the only time you ever looked right at me. Something I waited all of high school to experience. I never imagined it would turn out so bad and yet feel so good."

"What?" Quin stopped the rest of the words that wanted to tumble out. He didn't want her to stop, but he wasn't sure she had even heard him. She was so focused on her hands and yet lost in her own thoughts.

"I promise this is the only one I ever had, regardless of those silly rumors that circulated around school. I had a huge crush on you like the rest of the female population. This picture is the only evidence of giving into it. When I saw it, I knew I had to have it printed. I had to have it to remind me of the split second when I was the center of your attention. Those few precious seconds when the joy of being noticed coursed through me. But I also needed it to remind me that with the good comes the bad. The teasing and taunting from the popular kids, your indifference when you'd walk by me in the halls, and the hell of those last few months of school almost made those seconds not worth it.

At some point, after school ended, I was able to turn those negatives into a positive. I used those painful moments to see things differently through the lens and became a better photographer. I also decided I wouldn't let them define me.

I did my best to put myself out there more and start living on the other side of the camera. That experience, that one moment in time, shaped who I am today. At least that's what I think. So I guess, in a way, I should say thank you."

She looked up at him and he realized she was serious. "I'm not going to say you're welcome."

Her forehead scrunched in confusion. He raised his hand to stop any argument that might come out of her mouth. "Now wait, it's my turn. You need to hear me out."

Quin got up from his seat and walked over to Laurel. Grabbing up her hand, he looked back at the uncomfortable futon. No way was he getting back on that thing. He pulled her out into the living room where they could be more comfortable, he hoped. She may have turned that experience around and was pretty much over it, but guilt still weighed on him. He pushed her down to the couch, taking a seat next to her. Gathering her hands in his again, he kissed the backs before resting their hands on his thigh.

"I'm sorry all of that ever happened. I regretted what I said the second it was out of my mouth. I wanted to apologize but never had the nerve. The more time that went by, the harder it got. At some point I figured it would be better to ignore you and just move forward, but I never forgot the tears in your eyes as you rushed off. I never forgot the girl I hurt and it killed me in some way. My Momma raised her boys better than to treat a woman like that. My only excuse, and it's a lame one, is that I was a teenager too full of myself."

"I know that. Well, not about you being sorry, but I knew the teenage boy thing. We were all kinda young and dumb. It's easy to look back now and say it wasn't so bad. The whole point of the story wasn't to get you to say you're sorry, but I have to admit, it's nice to hear. My point was that when I ran across the new picture of you from yesterday, it reminded me of the one from years ago. I dug it out and, I don't know, was seeing how you've changed. In personality and...."

Her words ended abruptly as she chewed on her lip. Quin wanted to lean over and lave the abused area with his tongue but he sat as still as he could, only indulging in rubbing circles on the smooth skin of her hands with his thumbs. They needed to get everything out in the open. Have a clean slate in order to move forward, which he found he desperately wanted to do. When she didn't go on he prompted her. "And?"

Laurel glanced up at him. He watched as heat built, deepening the green of her eyes. "And physically," she whispered.

Well, damn! "And what did you see that changed in me?" Not that he was fishing for compliments, but he wondered if she saw him for the man he turned into or if she was still thinking of the boy he used to be.

"Well, when it comes to physical, I can see you're bigger and more defined than you were in high school. Your shoulders are broader, muscles much more defined." She glanced away quickly before looking him in the face again. "I couldn't help but notice when you had your shirt off that morning at the Shack." Laurel pulled one of her hands free and he found he missed the contact. She lightly touched the bridge of his nose and ran her finger over it as she spoke. "You've also broken your nose. You're face has thinned out and you have a more rugged, manly look." Her fingers glanced over his forehead and cheekbones before caressing his jaw. The touch was so light it felt like butterflies were racing over his face.

She leaned forward, close enough he could feel her hot, sweet breath on his lips. He ached to close the distance but was curious to see what she would do next. So far she'd only talked about his physical appearance and, from the soft, husky sound of her voice, she liked how he looked. "You're lips look to be the same—oh so tempting and kissable." Exhaling the last word she bent forward, sucking his bottom lip into her mouth.

That was the end of his control. He gathered her up, pulling her over his body, arranging her legs on the outside of his. When he pulled her down onto his erection, the heat emanating from her pussy was almost too much to take. She wiggled on top of him, forcing him to grab her hips to keep her still.

He didn't know why but something stopped him from taking it further. Breaking away from her lips, he dropped his head onto the back of the couch and counted to ten…twice.

While his body was primed for action, his brain, the one actually in his head, needed to know if she was interested in only the outside façade or if she was just living a teenage girl's fantasy with the boy he used to be?

Lifting his head he opened his eyes zeroing in on her face. "Honey, we need to slow down."

Laurel tilted her head to the side, her brows furrowed and lips thinned. "You don't want me?"

"Now I didn't say that. I said we needed to slow down. I am more than ready to make love to you while you're wrapped around me but, for some damned reason, I want to know you're doing it for the right reason."

"And I'm going to guess you being hot and me being horny isn't the right reason?"

Quin's heart dropped, she only wanted him for his looks. He went to move her off his lap but she grabbed onto the back of the couch, squeezed her legs against his thighs and wouldn't let go. "Laurel, please. I need to know you want the man and not the teenaged boy you had a crush on. It's important to me."

When she wouldn't move, Quin dropped his head back again and shut his eyes. Eventually, she would have to get up and move; at least that's what he was trying to convince himself of. It would help too if he could will away the painful erection pressing against his zipper and ignore the feel of her draped over him. The little voice that belonged to the horny guy inside his head told him he was crazy for stopping before things really got started.

The feel of soft lips touched first one cheek, then the other. "You want to know what kind of man I think you are now?"

Raising his head he looked at her warily. "Sure."

"An honorable one. You work hard, you play hard and you make sure everyone around you is taken care of. You're thoughtful and protective of your family and friends. You consider things before you speak and would never do anything that might cause hurt feelings. You've grown up, just like I have, and I like the man I see. Is there a part of me that still has a crush on that boy? Yes. Do I know I'm with the man he became? Definitely. You've shocked the hell out of me with all of the attention. It goes straight to my heart when you hold my hand just because you want to. You seem interested in my work and in my life. It makes me think you might be interested in more than just a quick fuck. That maybe you might be interested in more than just a one-night stand."

"I am." He was quick to affirm what she said because he *was* interested in more. Spending time with her outside the bedroom was fantastic. Granted, he was sure once they got to the bedroom things would explode, but this one-on-one quality time stuff…well, it blew his mind. The fact that earlier he suggested not having sex and just spending time with her made him think there really was something special about her. He knew, in his heart, he needed to cultivate the relationship.

The oddest revelation smacked him upside the head. He was finally ready for something that would last and he was sure that something would be with her. "And because I am interested in more, you my dear, are going to have to get off my lap. Let's get to work on that book like we planned and I vaguely recall you offering up dinner."

The brilliant smile that graced Laurel's lips made the throbbing ache in his groin worth it. She started to shift off his lap but not before snagging one more kiss. He really hoped this was going to the place he thought it might.

Chapter Eight

Warm sunlight coming through her bedroom window pulled Laurel from the best night's sleep she'd had to date. Stretching her limbs, it wasn't until she tried to roll onto her back that she realized she wasn't alone in bed. The arm around her waist tightened and she became fully aware of the erection pressing against her ass.

Oh no! What did I do? Taking a peek over her shoulder, she wasn't quite sure how to react. Quin Ferris was in bed with her. She wiggled a little and from the feel of things, neither of them was naked.

The night before rushed back to her. They had stayed up late into the evening eating pizza, drinking wine, talking and working on the book. When they finished with everything, she decided there was no way she was letting him drive home, not even when he said he was fine. No drinking and driving on her watch!

Since she insisted he stay, he insisted they share her queen-sized bed, stating he would never fit on the couch. Inside, she'd done a little dance at the hope that he had changed his mind from earlier about not having sex. Stripping down to her tank top and panties, she climbed in bed followed by Quin wearing only his boxers but, once their heads hit the pillows, they were both out like a light.

The hand snaking its way up to her breast pulled her from her musings.

"Morning honey. That's some awfully loud thinking you've got going on." Quin placed a kiss on her shoulder the same moment his nimble fingers grasped her tightening nipple. He plucked and pulled, alternating between breasts, before pulling a moan from her core.

"Hmm…not thinking anymore."

"Good. That was the idea."

More kisses landed on her exposed shoulder before he worked his wicked mouth up her neck. Rolling slightly she met his lips with her own and, like the night before, he was gentle, slowly increasing the pressure while bringing up her temperature.

"So, about that no sex thing," he rumbled against her lips.

"Yeah?" It was the only coherent thing she could come up with just then. Lust and need were spiraling through her preventing any other thoughts.

"I'd like to change my mind."

"Thank goodness!" When she went to roll onto her side, he quickly maneuvered her to the middle of the bed and underneath him, centering his erection on the mound between her open thighs. He pushed up her tank top, not waiting for it to be off completely before latching onto her breast. Licking and sucking her nipple to a hard point while his fingers plucked at the other. He bit down, sending pain and pleasure on a one-way path straight to her sex. She tilted her hips to grind her clit against the hard ridge of his penis. It was enough to fuel the fire burning inside but not enough to make her come.

"Damn honey, you feel good beneath me."

"I think it would be even better if we got rid of the rest of our clothes?"

Quin grinned up at her. "Sounds like a great idea."

Instead of letting her up, he shimmied down her body, kissing her ribs along the way to the spot just above her neatly trimmed pussy.

"I'd like a snack first."

A snack? He was hungry? Her thoughts were quickly washed away in a flood of sensation. Quin's mouth settled on her pussy, the thin piece of cotton blocking him from her delicate skin. He didn't seem to mind, though, when he ran his tongue the length of her pussy, pushing the material into her folds. A low hum of approval vibrated from him when arousal spilled from within, dampening the cloth even more.

"How much do you like these panties?"

Her mind was too numb with pleasure; surely she couldn't have heard him correctly.

Before she could say anything to the contrary, he snapped the thin elastic band on one side followed by the other. "Never mind, I'll get you new ones if they were your favorite."

Pushing his nose into her mound he took a deep breath. "Damn honey, you smell delicious." Swiping his tongue through her, she about bounced him off the bed. "Taste even better."

Slowly he worked her over. First, fucking her with that devil's tongue while rubbing small circles over her clit with his thumb. Her arousal spiked when he drew the tip of his tongue up to the sensitive nub while inserting two long fingers into her channel. Laving the tortured flesh, he sucked it between his lips, curved his fingers inside her and hit that magic spot she'd never been able to find on her own or with any other man.

A strangled cry escaped her lips as he pressed just enough to send shockwaves through her nerves. Her hand flew to his head grabbing his hair to keep him in place as she rode the orgasm out. Only letting up when tiny tremors were all that was left.

Quin lifted from between her legs, hands bracketing her hips, he placed a soft kiss on her belly. "Beautiful."

Laurel grabbed him by the ears and pulled him to her until he was within kissing distance. She plunged her tongue into his mouth, shivering in delight when she tasted her essence.

"I need to be in you honey. Are you ready for that?"

"Definitely." She hooked her legs around his back, guiding him to her center. Right before the tip of his shaft made contact, he pulled back.

"Condom."

"Oh! I don't have any." She felt heat rise in her cheeks. "I don't have men over so I don't have any here."

Dropping a kiss on her nose, he bounded out of bed. "Where are my pants? I wasn't sure what was going to happen when I came over, but I wanted to be prepared."

Tilting her head to the side she ogled his firm ass as he bent down to grab the garment off the floor. Digging into one of the cargo pockets, Quin pulled out a strip of condoms. Turning back toward her, he must have seen the surprise on her face when she saw what he was holding. The corner of his mouth curved up in that lady-killer smile that melted her panties every time.

"That's more than being prepared. That's hoping for a marathon sex session," she said.

Quin chuckled, climbing back on the bed. He tore a condom off the pack, tossing the rest on the nightstand. Tearing open the foil, he rolled the latex over his erection, dragging his hand down the impressive length. Eyes locked onto the movement, her pussy quivered in anticipation.

"Honey?" Quin's deep voice snagged her attention.

"Hmm?"

"If you don't stop staring at me like that, I won't be able to go slow and take my time like I want."

Without thought she nibbled on her bottom lip, the action seeming to snap any restraint he had left in him.

Covering her body, Quin pressed forward until the blunt head of his cock notched in the entrance of her pussy. "I warned you," he growled.

"I never told you to go slow. I want to see you come unleashed Quin." She wasn't sure why, but she wanted to taunt him with her words.

Slamming his mouth onto hers, their tongues tangled as they devoured each other. Quin tunneled inside her in one powerful thrust, knocking the air from her lungs.

"So fucking tight." Quin grunted, pulling out before snapping his hips forward again, setting up a quick, hard rhythm. Her hips rolled forward creating more friction as the base of his shaft bumped into her clit. Ecstasy wound through her and all she cared about was reaching the orgasm building up inside.

Slipping her hand down between their bodies, she gathered the moisture from around Quin's shaft. Placing her index finger on her clit added that extra bit of pressure she needed. In a blur her orgasm hit, her eyelids slammed shut as sparks exploded. Crying out Quin's name, she was vaguely aware of him picking up speed, shuttling his hips back and forth, the rhythm uneven. Within seconds he joined her in the frenzy, shooting hot come into the tip of the condom.

Breathing heavily Quin collapsed on top of her before rolling them onto their sides, still intimately connected. It was when he started to soften that he pulled out, holding the base of the condom to keep anything from leaking out. He placed a kiss on her lips before making his way to the bathroom. A couple of minutes later, he was crawling back into bed with her. Turning her body so her back was to his chest, wrapping himself around her. She felt safe and protected in his arms. Like she was meant to be right where she was.

Neither said a word as the world starting revolving again, too content to want to break the spell around them.

Drifting in and out of sleep, Laurel jolted to awareness when her name escaped Quin's lips as he dozed behind her.

A glance at the clock and she about had a heart attack. She had forty minutes to get showered and dressed before she needed to meet her parents for brunch.

"Quin!" He grumbled next to her but didn't move. She glanced at him, at some point they had shifted apart. His tanned, defined chest was bare. Tempting her to trace the bumps and dips of his physique. She needed to snap out of it. "Quin! We have to get up."

"I don't think I can go again honey, but thanks for the ego boost." He rolled onto his side and pulled her against him.

"Not that! I have to get cleaned up. I'm supposed to meet my parents for brunch, remember?"

"Your parents? Oh yeah. That's why we couldn't get together Sunday."

"Today is Sunday. It'll take me at least ten minutes to get to the other side of town where the restaurant is, so let's go." She peeled his arm away from her waist and shot out of bed, making a mad dash to the bathroom. Quin walked in a couple steps behind her chuckling.

"Babe, you need to slow down." He grabbed her by the shoulders and stopped her from moving. "Give me a second and I'll get the shower going. Why don't you grab us some towels."

"Us?"

"Yes, us. I need a shower too. I don't want your parents smelling sex on me when I meet them. What kind of first impression would that make?"

"Meet them?" She sounded like a parrot, knew she was dumbly repeating him, but he had said it was too soon to meet her parents.

Quin pressed a kiss to her lips. "Yes. I want to meet them. I hate to tell you but you aren't getting rid of me that easily. Besides, I'd rather they know now that I plan on marrying you when you're ready."

"Hold on there. Marry me? Isn't it a bit soon to be talking about marriage?" She probed inward to see how she felt about that and decided she rather liked the idea. It was still too soon, but she felt lightness in her heart at the thought of being with him forever.

Quin was her dream guy. Always had been. While teenage Quin was a sight to behold, she much preferred the grown up version. She wasn't lying to him the night before when she said she liked the man he had turned into. Along with everything else she told him, there was a funny, quirky side she adored as well as a romantic, sweet side you wouldn't guess was there. She never would have pictured Quin, the football stud, content with sitting around watching silly horror movies or trading stories about his family just to get to know a woman better.

"Yeah, I know it's soon but I feel it here." He pulled her hand up to his bare chest, placing it over his heart. "I knew that first time I saw you, you were special."

"You mean out at the jump that first day?" *Because he couldn't mean back in high school.*

"No, I mean the first time I really saw you. That day out on the field."

Laurel was stunned into silence.

"Honey, you okay?" She looked at Quin, startled to find him looking at her with concern. "You aren't freaking out on me are you?"

She couldn't help but laugh or the prick of tears in her eyes. "I'm freaking out a little, but I'll be fine. Let's get cleaned up. I'd love for you to meet my parents." Stepping into the shower she pulled Quin in behind her. Excitement coursed through her soul. Quin really and truly wanted to be with her. Forever.

THE END

About Brandy Walker

As a teenager Brandy would spend time at her Nana and Papa's writing angst filled stories of unrequited love. All revolving around whatever cute boy she had a crush on at the time. The stories, which no longer exist, were a way to get out the emotions bottled up inside. After a time her interests changed and writing got left behind.

After rediscovering her love of reading, romance to be specific, story ideas starting popping up in her head. With some prodding from her friends she decided to try her hand at writing romance and has written around ten stories in various states of completion. With a plan in place she's hoping to bring more of her stories to life.

Brandy is a Navy brat, prior enlisted Army, current Army wife, and mom. She lives in Washington State with her husband of 18 years, three kids and one dog.

email | brandy@brandywalker.net
Website | www.brandywalker.net
Twitter | www.twitter.com/Brandy_W
Facebook | www.facebook.com/brandywalkerfanpage

The follow up to Caught in the Moment is now available.

Read Kegen's story in...

Fly Guy Next Door

Freefall, Book 2

Marlowe Scott is living the dream. She bought her first house, opened Whispers, a lingerie boutique, and is seeing her hot next-door neighbor Kegen Ferris. The only hang-up in this ideal life…she's falling for Kegen harder and faster than she thought possible. She's not sure that's the best move she's ever made.

Skydiving is easier than falling in love...

Please enjoy this excerpt from Chapter One

Standing on the front porch waiting for her friend Steph to show up, Marlowe Scott was currently indulging in one of her favorite new pastimes. Drooling over the visual treat that was Kegen and Revlin Ferris.

They knew she was watching them. What red-blooded woman wouldn't be? They were toned, tanned, and completely and utterly scrumptious. Both sporting long, curling at the edges black hair. Glimmering dark brown eyes that, when focused on you, tried to lure you into doing something naughty. And they both had the same dragonfly infinity knot and matching intricate Celtic band tattoo.

Marlowe couldn't hold back the giggle that escaped. Twins with twin tattoos, how cute, even though absolutely nothing about them could be construed as such. She knew the meaning behind it but it still made her laugh, well...giggle really.

Rev explained they picked the dragonfly because of its speed and grace flying through the air. They identified with it when they jumped out of an airplane, experiencing the rush of the freefall dive while gliding through the air. Marlowe didn't want to inflate his or Kegen's ego more than they already were by telling them it didn't matter what design was etched into his or his twin's skin; anything would look good on them. All she said was that it was very nice. Fitting for what they did in their daily lives.

Her gaze swept over Kegen, taking in every delicious inch of him as he walked around the back of his huge black and gray truck. He was her special treat. The man she wanted more and more with each passing day.

He easily topped her five feet four frame by at least eight inches. She absolutely loved it. Tall men were her weakness. She loved exploring, tasting and teasing their towering bodies from head to toe. Something she had done the first time she got Kegen naked and tied down to her bed. He called it torture, but she knew he loved every minute of it. He moaned and bucked beneath her as she nipped at his skin before sucking or licking the offended spots.

Kegen looked her way, a sly, knowing grin kicking up one corner of his mouth. Pulling his dark blue shirt off, he used it to wipe down his

B
O
N
U
S

lightly furred chest before stuffing the tail of it into the back pocket of his black cargo shorts. He winked at her before turning his attention back to the Tonneau cover, popping it open with ease.

Marlowe had to fan herself as heat rose over her chest, neck and face. Good gracious that man was gorgeous. The thick tattoo wrapped around his right bicep rippled as the muscles in his arms bulged and flexed. What she wouldn't give to go to him, run her hands up his arms, and feel the strength and power within. To kiss and lick the light salty taste left on his skin after a long day at work. She wanted to pull him against her body and feel how much he wanted her. Have him lift her onto the tailgate of the truck and spread her willing thighs open. Fit them together until his hard cock pressed against her needy pussy.

A shiver of excitement raced down her spine as arousal rippled through her. Her nipples puckered into tight knots. The need to head inside and masturbate warred with her need to feel his body next to hers. It was almost too much to handle. But resist she would. She didn't doubt any move on her part would feed Kegen's male pride. The knowledge that he could work her into a frenzy without even touching her would inflating that ego more.

Rev sauntered out of the house wearing similar black cargo shorts and a grey Chute Shack tank top. Too caught up in lusting after his brother, she barely noticed when he smiled and waved in her direction. His deep chuckle floated across their shared lawns, pulling her from the sexual haze she was in.

Marlowe had the decency to blush at being caught staring. That wasn't the first time she had gotten sidetracked by Kegen. It probably wouldn't be the last either. She adored him body and soul.

A sudden frown formed on her face, pulling the corners of her mouth down.

Adored him.

Now there was the understatement of the century. They had been seeing each other for a little over three months and she already adored him. What was next, loving him? Wanting to spend the rest of her life with him?

A moment's panic knotted her stomach. Her heart whispered yes while her, at times, commitment-phobic mind screamed no.

Read more about Marlowe and Kegen to find out how Marlowe falls for the FLY GUY NEXT DOOR. Available in print and digital at your favorite online bookstores.

Tiger Nip Series

Craving More, Book One
TEZ Publishing

Corrine Hart is ready for a few days off for rest and relaxation. At the top of her to-do list is spending as much time as possible in tiger form and doing her best to banish all thoughts of the mysterious *Hunky Cupcake Guy* who spent the last two weeks driving her libido insane.

Jett Montgomery-Murphy just wants to know if the tasty treats that keep showing up at work are the same ones his best friend used to get while they were in college. a trip to *Sweet Confections* confirms what he thought and brings him in close contact with the one woman he's secretly lusted after for years, his best friend's sister Corrine.

A late night tryst leads to two tigers finding their mates and two humans unsure what to do next. Add in an overbearing brother, a best friend with her own drama, and a crazy ex-girlfriend that has a checkered past and you have a recipe for disaster.

Will Corrine and Jett be able to overcome the unexpected obstacles on their way to falling in love? Or will they throw in the towel before the relationship even gets off the ground?

What happens when you find yourself craving more....

Please enjoy this excerpt from Chapter One.

Corrine Hart ambled up the slope behind her sprawling two-story home. The rush of endorphins from the evening run settled in her system, sending pinpricks of sensation along her skin, the hairs lifting on the back of her neck. It was a feeling she would never tire of. The only thing that would have made it better was if her best friend in the entire world had been running next to her, hanging out like they usually did on a quiet Friday night. De-stressing from their hectic workweek before starting it all over again.

Sadly, her friend had been summoned home, and one thing MJ and Corrine never did was disobey their parents. Family was number one in both their lives.

In all honesty, it was probably best MJ wouldn't be around the next couple of days. Corrine's twin brother, Sampson, called earlier in the day and announced he would be there in the morning. Corrine wasn't in the mood to deal with the chemistry that always vibrated between the two of them. Not that MJ or Sam would ever admit to the attraction, and it didn't help that her friend couldn't say a single nice thing to Sam, or that he either acted oblivious to her presence or teased her unmercifully. It was always one extreme or the other. Never a happy medium.

Yeah, it was better this way. She was all for *less* stress right now. In an unprecedented move, she decided to shut the bakery down for the long weekend and take some much-needed time for herself.

Letting out a snort, Corrine plopped down in the grass and stretched her limbs before settling into the soothing task of grooming her front right paw. With each swipe of her tongue; her best friend, brother, the bakery, and every other nagging thought and task drifted from her mind.

Minutes passed by in complete silence, the repetitive motion calming her frazzled nerves. Eventually there was nothing left to groom and Corrine was finally able to enjoy the scenery. Off to the right, she could just make out the fuzzy shape of her neighbor's home in the distance. Close enough if there was trouble, still far enough away as to not disturb him. A look to the left, and the wooded area came to life as a warm breeze wound its way through the trees; limbs swaying and beckoning her to come play.

This was why she moved to Cascade, Colorado. The peace and quite of the woods mixed with a homey midtown feel. Open spaces mingling with shops galore. What every female shifter could ask for.

Corrine rolled onto her side, resting her head on the cool grass. Eyes closed, muscles relaxed she was almost asleep when the image of a man flashed into her head.

Short brown hair she ached to run her fingers through. Golden flecked nut-brown eyes that melted her insides when they locked onto her. Plus there was his sexy as sin smile that crooked up on one side, drawing attention to his full lower lip.

A purr rolled from her throat as she imagined him skimming his lips over her body. Stopping at her aching breasts for excruciating seconds before gliding lower.

At over six-feet tall, the mystery man was built like a hard-edged linebacker: broad shoulders, thick muscular arms and legs, and she'd bet the bakery he had abs of steel. It would take her days to kiss and explore every inch of his sun-kissed skin. Days she would happily give up to do just that.

She was dying to find out if he tasted as good as he smelled. Even now, when she took a deep breath, she could swear she smelled his rich, spicy musk. It had to be from her run-in with him earlier in the day and the lingering memories dancing through her head.

He visited the bakery in the flesh during the day and invaded her dreams at night. She was never able to get him out of her thoughts. Not that she tried very hard. She was more than happy to let him worship her body, if only in her imagination.

He was the kind of guy she fantasized about meeting and falling in love with. Too bad any time he was near, her knees went weak and her tongue refused to work. Not to mention the most she got out of him was a wink and a smile. For two weeks she had been a frustrated bundle of nerves on the verge of snapping. No amount of masturbation would make the ache for him go away, and damn it all—she tried her best to make that happen. She probably needed to replace the batteries in her favorite vibrator—again.

Claiming More, Book 2
TEZ Publishing

Sampson Hart has known **Mary Jane Poppy** for ten years. She's his sister's best friend, business partner, and has had a crush on Sam for years. When the mating pull hits him, he's ready to claim her as his own. Given their history, it should be simple. Right?

MJ has loved Sam since she was fifteen. But being a hybrid, she's been told all her life she won't have a mate. When Sam proclaims she belongs to him, she doesn't believe it; the mating pull isn't there, and Sam isn't meant to be hers.

Running back home to escape the love she feels for Sam, MJ agrees to become the companion of a man who lost his mate and has three young children to raise. It is the only way to set Sam free to find the one he is truly meant to be with.

Will Sam be claiming more or will the one he desires most find comfort in the arms of another?

Dallas & Kacie : Tiger Bite, Book 2.5
TEZ Publishing

BONUS

It's the holiday season and **Kacie Cook** is counting down the hours until its time to close up *Sweet Confections*. Not that she had any great plans for the week the bakery is closed. She won't be seeing her family—yet again, and all of her friends are too busy. All she had planned is a little rest and relaxation. That is until the last customer of the night walks in. Could he be the one to bring some holiday cheer and possibly change her life forever?

The Tiger Bite is a short story featuring Kacie Cook, an employee at Sweet confection, and Dallas Andersen, the younger brother of Devon Andersen who appears in Claiming More.

If you're just looking for something to give you a glimpse of my Tiger Nip world then this is a good place to start, though I feel the books should be read in order to get the most enjoyment out of it.

Next up in the Tiger Nip Series....

Finding More

Tiger Nip, Book 3

(Unedited, work in progress)

Chapter One

Devon Andersen jogged back up the brick path to his house, unlocking the front door to find Sebastian's backpack sitting right where he left it…next to the door. Shaking his head at forgetting the necessary item, he snatched it up, relocked the door and made his way back to his SUV.

One would think he would be used to getting the kids ready for the day at this point, almost two years after his wife's death.

The big black Lincoln with the latest and greatest in safety features was filled with his most precious cargo—his kids. Marcus, his oldest at seven years old and who had his window down, sat next to his baby brother, three-year-old Sebastian chatting. Tabitha, his five-year-old daughter and the spitting image of his late wife, sat on the other side of Sebastian attempting to read a story amid the boys constant talk.

Devon climbed into the driver's side, tossing the backpack onto the passenger seat. "Found it. You guys ready to go?" He peered into the backseat, double-checking the kids were strapped into their seats.

"We've been ready," Tabitha piped up, not bothering to look up from her book.

God it killed him every time he looked at her. Not in a bad way but in a way that made his heart ache at their loss. Tabitha was a tiny version of her mother. Quiet and well behaved. She did as she was told without argument. Tabitha had the same slim, fragile build to her. Even though she had the same midnight black hair as Devon, her eyes were all her mother's. All of the kids had their mother's eyes. Bright green, like a lush forest that danced with the rays of the sun.

Sadness gripped his heart as the oxygen got stopped up in his lungs. He forced himself to exhale. To keep breathing and go on like he had since the day of the accident.

He lost his mate. His children lost their mother. A beautiful woman who dedicated each and every waking moment to them. They would never again feel her kissed goodnight after she sang a lullaby. Turning the lights out and whispering *my eternal love* into the quiet of the room.

She would never be able to kiss their boo-boos, soothe their hurt feelings, or see their first shifts. She would never see them grow into rambunctious teenagers and help guide them through life.

"Dad, we're gonna be late for school," Marcus insisted, pulling Devon from his depressing thoughts.

Devon looked at the clock on the dash, startled to see the time. *Shit, I'm going to be late for work.* "I'm on it, son."

Throwing the SUV into reverse he backed down the long driveway and out into the street. It took him ten minutes to get across town to the school Marcus and Tabitha went to. When he pulled up front, in the drop-off zone, Marcus's door swung open and he hopped out before Devon had a chance to open his own.

"See ya later Dad. Love you." Marcus slammed the door and ran inside without a glance back. Already Marcus was pulling away it seemed. That shouldn't happen when a kid was seven.

Shaking his head Devon walked around the front of the SUV and opened Tabitha's door. She leaned over and kissed Sebastian on the cheek before climbing out. She clutched his hand and his heart tugged in response. The first day of school had been hard on them both. Tabitha didn't want to leave her little brother, so used to spending her days with him at home with the nanny or in the on-sight daycare at the hospital. She was afraid she wouldn't make friends because she was so quiet.

Hell, he was afraid of the same things for her. Without her mom around, Tabitha withdrew into her little shell. She wouldn't speak and she wouldn't leave his side. It took almost six months of therapy to get her to talk again. To find out she was petrified she would lose him just like she lost her mommy.

She was doing better now. She made friends in Kindergarten, talked, and smiled more. There were still moments like now when she had to walk into the school.

They walked around the SUV and to his door. Tabitha tugged on his hand. He knelt down next to her.

"Do you want me to walk you to the door sweetpea?"

"No Daddy, its okay. The teacher is right there." She wrapped her skinny little arms around his neck and squeezed. "You have a good day, Daddy." She kissed him on the cheek.

He hugged her back. "You have a good day too. You sure you don't want me to walk you to the door."

Tabitha's gaze slid to the teacher waiting, holding the door open, then back to him. "I'll be okay."

Letting go, she adjusted her backpack and serenely walked to the open door. She turned at the last minute and blew him a kiss before gong inside.

The teacher holding the door waved, shutting the door as she followed Tabitha inside.

Devon sighed. *How in the hell did Sasha do this every day?* He loved seeing his children happy and healthy and anxious to go to school. A piece of him broke every time he watched them walk away though. His babies were growing up and he was the only one around to see it. The only parent to share in the joys and heartbreak.

"Dad you're going to be late for work. Miss Crabtree is going to get mad at you," Sebastian said from inside the SUV.

Devon climbed back into the driver's seat and grinned at his youngest son. "Miss Crabtree won't be mad that I'm a little late. She works for daddy, so it will be fine. Should I bring her a cookie just in case?"

Sebastian giggled. "She doesn't like cookies. She likes fat brownies."

Devon's eyebrows shot up. That was news to him. "Are you sure we're talking about Miss Crabtree and not you?"

Sebastian shrugged and smiled. "We can get both."

Leave it to a three year old to come up with a solution. Devon chuckled and pulled away from the curb. "Cookies and brownies it is. We'll hit the drive through at Cuppa Claire's, sound good?"

"Yay!" Sebastian clapped his hands gleefully.

Devon hauled Sebastian, Sebastian's backpack (because he wouldn't put it on), Devon's own briefcase, and their overstuffed Cuppa Claire's bag through the parking garage and into the hospital. It was a good thing he forgot to order the coffee he wanted. He didn't have any hands left to carry it.

The first sight that greeted him as they passed through the sliding door was Miss Crabtree, the on-site daycare supervisor.

"You're late Dr. Andersen. What have I told you about that? You need to have the kids on a good schedule. You *need* to be seeing your patients—on time. No one likes to be left waiting." She held out her arms ready to receive Sebastian and all of his things.

He handed her the backpack but when he went to shift his son to her Sebastian wiggled and insisted he get down. "I can walk."

Devon wished the kid had said *that* ten minutes ago when they were trudging through the parking lot. Fishing inside the Cuppa Claire's bag he pulled out another smaller bag, then handed the big bag over. He kissed the sixty-year-old Miss Crabtree on the cheek. "You're the best Mary. Don't let those other doctors tell you any different."

Miss Crabtree blushed even as she tried to hold the stern look on her face. "You're the only one I have a problem with. Now scoot. Off you go and get to work. Young mister Andersen and I have things to do."

Devon saluted her, kissed Sebastian on the head, and then turned to walk toward his office.

The more distance between him and his son, the more he felt his doctor's mask fall into place. He let his worries about the kids fall to the wayside and concentrated on what he had to do for the day.

Being a family physician and working in the hospital was almost his salvation. Everyday there was something new, something different to occupy his mind.

Today the twins he delivered during the Gathering eight months ago would be coming in for a check-up. The boys were doing fine now but at the time of the delivery too much had gone wrong. He kept a close eye on them, knowing the pain it would cause if something were to happen to them. The young couple would be devastated.

The wildflowers in bloom around town would no doubt bring in those unlucky shifters with allergies. He would have to make sure he slotted walk-in time over the week.

The list went on and by the time he reached his office, he was feeling more like the in control, competent physician people expected.

I hope you enjoyed this snippet of Finding More. Look for it at your favorite online bookstore.

Decadent ROAR
Decadent Publishing

The tales in Decadent Roar explore college life and beyond from the shapeshifter or were-shifter's point of view. What's it like to be away from the pack? What freedoms can be explored? What dangers lurk? Do you pledge a fraternity? What about a sorority? Does this college happen to have a shifter-only spot on Greek row? Through parties to mid-terms, to discovering who they are, characters in a Decadent Roar tale will take you on a journey through college love, the ups and the downs, and what happens when everything you thought you knew turns out to be even more difficult than you would have believed?

Shifted Plans
Shifter U, Book 1

(Blurb subject to tweaking)

Avery Hillman has one year of college left and once it's over she has plans, BIG plan. A job managing her family's medical practice, an apartment of her own, and a new life where she's the one in charge. No hovering family, no annoying siblings, and no mate to have to divide her time to be with.

Declan Weller has one more class to finish. One more thing he can cross off his ten-year plan. Once that is done he can transfer to the new job waiting for him and his new life. He isn't looking for his mate and as far as he's concerned, finding her can wait another two years.

The Fates have a plan of their own. One that includes throwing Avery and Declan in each other's path. It's high time those two found each other and learn the most important thing of all…sometimes plans need to shift.

Other Books by Brandy Walker

Tiger Nip
TEZ Publishing
Craving More, Book One
Claiming More, Book 2
Dallas & Kacie: Tiger Bite, Book 2.5

Box Set
Sinfully Supernatural Contains Craving More

Freefall
TEZ Publishing
Caught in the Moment
Fly Guy Next Door

Shifter U
Shifted Plans, Book One
Decadent ROAR, NA Paranormal
Coming Nov 2015 from *Decadent Publishing*

Future Books/Series

Finding More, Tiger Nip, Book 3 - TBD
Giving More, Tiger Nip, Book 4 - TBD
Seeing More, Tiger Nip, Book 5 - TBD

Captured by Color, Freefall, Book 3 - TBD
Revving Her Engine, Freefall, Book 4 - TBD
Spinning Out of Control, Freefall, Book 5 - TBD

Praetorian Guards Series - TBD
Mystic Zodiac Series - Starting Jan 2015

MYSTIC ZODIAC SERIES

BONUS

Starting January 2015
One book each month

January - *Angel - Thane*

February - *Goddess / God - Parvati*

March - *Shifter - Gideon*

April - *Nymph - Lisa*

May - *Fae / Faerie - Celeste*

June - *Witch - Willow*

July - *Siren - Amber*

August - *Dragon - Adrian*

September - *Djinn - Colby*

October - *Vampire - Lucas*

November - *Spirit - Mace*

December - *Demon - Falcon*

www.brandywalker.net/bookshelf/mysticzodiac
www.facebook.com/mysticzodiacseries

www.ingramcontent.com/pod-product-compliance
Lightning Source LLC
Chambersburg PA
CBHW030238180626
46810CB00008B/3192